Laird of Her Heart

Book One in the Dundragon Time Travel Trilogy

When Maggie Spencer is mysteriously transported to the Scotland of her ancestors, she is stunned to come face to face with him. Dominic Dundragon, the man she's been half in love with her whole life. A man who's been dead for 700 years.

They both have enemies aplenty. Will she have a chance to win his love, or will this adventure end in disaster?

Laird of her Heart

SABRINA YORK

Laird of Her Heart
ISBN #: 978-1-941497-21-0
©Copyright Sabrina York 2015
Cover Design by Dar Albert
Edited by WriteRightEdits

LAIRD OF HER HEART

Dedication

This book is dedicated to Dar.

CHAPTER ONE

"WHAT ARE YOU STARING AT?"

Maggie Spencer snapped the book shut and glared at her cousin. "Nothing." How could she admit she'd been mooning over a man who'd been dead 700 years?

But seriously, he was hot. At least the sketch of him was. It had captured his bulging muscles, his piercing eyes and the ferocious beauty of his features. Something in his expression—the intensity of it, perhaps—utterly captivated her attention. He was exactly what she thought, imagined, dreamed a hot highlander of old would be.

Even his name was fascinating. Dominic. Dominic Dundragon, infamous Laird of the Macintosh Clan of Dar. It broke her heart that, at the age of 27, he'd been betrayed by a kinsman and killed in the Urquhart Ambush—a brutal slaughter of Chattan Lairds instigated by a rival clan. But again, it was a pointless grief. Even if he had lived to be a hundred, he'd still be dead now. Would have been dead for centuries.

Jenny tipped her head to the side to read the cover of Maggie's book and she grimaced. "That one again?"

Maggie sniffed and leaned back in her lawn chair. It was a lovely day in Seattle, a rare opportunity to soak up the sun and read. "It's a good book."

"It's a boring book."

"History is not boring. Besides, this is *our* family history. You should find it fascinating." Maggie did. "These are the events, the peoples that made us what we are."

"Ug. Dusty details. Wars. Famines. Plagues."

"Romances. Adventures." Handsome heroes. Could she not see it? The feud between the Camerons and the Macintoshes itself was fascinating reading. "Besides, Grandma wrote it. The least you could do is pretend to be interested. For her sake."

"That's not fair."

Maggie winced at the wounded thread in Jenny's tone. She hadn't meant to be hurtful. She traced the old binding with idle fingers. "Do you think she's okay?"

Jenny shrugged. "She wanted to go. She seems happy there." It was never easy, locking someone you loved away in a nursing home. Although, to be fair, Grandma wasn't locked away. She was probably playing BINGO with her minions. And winning. If not that, rumbling around town in the VRV van on one of the many tours the activity director dreamed up. Or eating pie. Valhalla Retirement Village, apparently, had excellent pie. And Grandma did love her pie.

Still, it had been hard moving her out of this rambling house she'd called home for over sixty years, into a tiny room in the nominal care wing of an assisted living community. "It's weird being here without her."

All Maggie's memories of this place included Grandma and Grandpa and cousins and Christmases. But Grandma had wanted them to stay. Insisted they keep the house. As though she couldn't bear the thought of strangers sitting on this patio, or cooking in her kitchen.

"It is weird." Jenny sighed. "But she seems happy."

Maggie nibbled on her lip. "I'm worried about her." Over there, in a strange place. Isolated. All alone.

"She seems happy." Yes, Jenny was the Redundancy Queen of Redundancy.

"But she's started giving her stuff away." Maggie fingered the locket at her neck.

"She could hardly keep it all. Her room is...smallish."

"You know what I mean." Maggie lifted a shoulder. "When elderly people start cleaning house..."

"She's not going to die. Not for decades. She's strong as a horse. She'll probably outlive us all."

"I know. But I worry." They drifted into silence then, both wreathed in their own thoughts—of Grandma, of Grandpa who'd passed last winter, of the big house on the hill where they'd just taken up residence. Though Grandma has asked them to live here, it still felt like an infiltration, an invasion. This was and always would be Grandma and Grandpa's house.

When it all became too maudlin, Maggie sighed and gestured to Jenny's book. "So, what are you reading?"

Jenny shot a dismissive look at Maggie's *History of the Macintosh Clan of Dar*. "Something *interesting*."

"What is it?"

"Jacobs' treatise on his theories of space-time."

Maggie rolled her eyes. She turned her attention to the vista below, the sparkling waters of the Puget Sound beyond the rolling hills of the family estate. The sky was blue, the breeze gentle. She tried to focus on how pleasant it was. Because, yeah, she knew what was coming.

"Now *this* is fascinating."

"Is it?" Oh. She shouldn't have said anything. It only encouraged Jenny.

"The chapter I'm reading is about the effects of gravity on time. Isn't that an intriguing concept?"

Maggie leaned closer and peered at the book through squinty eyes, just to make a point. "Are you reading fiction?"

Jenny snorted.

"How could gravity have any effect on something with no mass?" She was hardly a science genius like her cousin, but that much seemed like simple logic.

"It does in a singularity." Jenny flipped a few pages. "Here. They've postulated time shifts close to a black hole. Stretches. Folds. Kind of makes me wonder if it could make time act like a wormhole, you know, bending it over on itself so you could make a temporal hop."

"You're making my brain hurt." But it was, at least, her *temporal* lobe.

Jenny shot her a trademark smirk. "You did ask what I was reading. And you have to admit, it is an interesting possibility."

"It's not a possibility at all. Not if you have to go through a black hole to travel through time. Correct me if I'm wrong, but wouldn't a black hole rip you apart, atom by atom, if you got too close?" Maggie huffed a sigh. "Honestly. What are they teaching you in science school?"

Jenny ignored her. She often did. Physicists were notoriously pretentious. "There's a chapter… Where is it?" More riffling pages. "Ah. He talks about sites here, on Earth, where gravity behaves differently than it does elsewhere."

"Oh joy. My boobs will be delighted."

A glare. "Point being—"

"Was there an actual point?"

"Point being…" Jenny frowned. "You made me forget my point."

"Must have been an enthralling point."

"I hate when you do that."

"It's hardly my fault I'm so scintillating I make people forget what they were saying." She made it a *point* to bat her lashes.

Jenny grumbled something beneath her breath and went back to her riffling. "Oh. Right. These gravitational aberrations."

"Of course." Maggie stifled a sigh. Or not.

"Many of the sites, like Stonehenge and Machu Picchu—"

"And the Oregon Vortex?" She tapped her lip. "Ah, but then, isn't all of Oregon a vortex?"

"Hush. They have excellent donuts and some of my best friends live in Oregon."

"I have friends in Oregon too—"

"*Anyway*…" Jenny shot her a quelling glare. "Many of these sites were considered sacred or magical in the days of yore." She patted Maggie's hand. "You should like that part. Days of yore were dusty."

Maggie made a face and opened her tome again to *that* page. Not to stare at him again, or anything like that.

He didn't look dusty. He looked strong and bold and handsome. Wild. Savage.

They didn't make men like that anymore.

Metrosexual, metroschmexual.

"Oh good googelymoogley," Jenny warbled. "Are you drooling over him again?"

"I do not drool."

"You do actually." And then she added in a not-very-aside aside, "You snore too."

"I most certainly do not snore."

"Last night I thought you were running a chainsaw in your room."

"As long as we're laying out our grievances—"

"Were we? I thought we were just stating facts."

"All right. Just stating facts. You might want to lay off the broccoli."

Jenny bristled. "Just what is that supposed to mean?"

"Nothing. Just sayin'."

"Are you intimating that I *fart*?"

"I think the scientific term is gaseous anomalies."

"I do not fart!"

"Just remember, in the winter, don't stand too close to the fireplace."

"I... What?"

Maggie exploded a hand. "Ker-blooey."

Jenny tried not to smile and failed. "You know what you are?"

"Awesome?" A, like, Valley girl cant.

"A wench. That's what you are."

"You love me and you know it."

"I do. But you're a wench." She narrowed her eyes. "And it's your turn to make dinner."

"I don't think I want to live with you after all."

"Because I insist that we share the household duties?"

"Oh, no, I was referring to the flatulence."

Jenny smacked her on the shoulder and chuckled. Then she sobered. "Seriously. It's your turn to make dinner."

Maggie grimaced. She hated cooking. With. A. Passion. "How about a salad?"

It was adorable the way Jenny's nose curled up. The way she hacked and gagged. "No. Not salad."

"If it's my turn to make dinner, I get to pick the food."

"Salad is not real food. Google it."

"I could put bacon on it..."

"Even so, not real food. How about pizza?"

"You want me to make pizza? Do you remember the last time I put something in the oven?" Although the fireman who had responded to the blaze had been cute.

"To be fair, that is a very old oven."

"It probably came with the house." The house was nearly a century old.

"Take-out then?"

Maggie hid her smile. She'd been angling for take-out all along. "Pizza?"

"With olives?"

It was Maggie's turn to hack and gag. "Olives are disgusting. Pineapple."

"Pineapple has no place on a pizza."

"My turn to cook, remember?"

"Making a phone call does not count as cooking."

"Okay. Half…" Shudder. "Olives and half pineapple?"

"Deal."

Maggie set aside her book and stood. As she headed across the porch, Jenny warbled, "And don't forget the anchovies!"

"Gross."

When she opened the door, something small and furry and white shot out, darted between her legs and fairly flew down the steps into the yard. "Shit," she muttered and let the screen door close. "Mop got out. Will you go get him?"

Jenny frowned at the dog as he disappeared into the woods. "*You* let him out."

"But I need to 'make dinner'." Total air quotes there.

"I'll call for pizza. You get the dog."

"Oh, all right." Maggie sighed and tramped back down the stairs. *Damn dog.* It was getting dark and the little twerp might get snatched by a coyote. Though they were technically in the Seattle city limits, their property was on a hill, surrounded by old growth forest for miles. Grandma and Grandpa had resisted all offers to buy them out. And with all the construction making incursions into their habitats, critters tended to flock to this forest. They'd even once spotted a bear.

Maggie had to go get him. He was Grandma's darling; she would be devastated if anything happened to him. But in all honesty, Grandma should have warned them he was an escape artist when she handed over the leash. He was named Mop because he looked like one with all that scraggly hair. Maybe they should *use* him as one.

Maggie sighed and set out for the woods, but turned back to waggle a finger at her cousin. "You better not forget the pineapples on that pizza."

Jenny's grin was disarming. "You better take a flashlight," she chirped. "Last time it took me a couple hours to find him."

* * *

Maggie was glad she'd brought the flashlight, because even though the sun was still sinking, once she got deep into the trees, it was hard to see. And Mop was small. Why old women went for the tiny yippy dogs was a mystery. In Maggie's mind it wasn't a real dog unless it could knock her down.

She shined the beam into the scrub and called him. "Mop? Moppie? I have nom noms for you." She didn't. It was a lie. But it hardly mattered since the stupid mutt didn't even speak English.

She heard a bark from her right, little more than a canine taunt. She growled to herself and forged off in that direction. And yeah, there he was, dancing around in circles. But when she neared, he took off again.

This happened several times, luring her deeper and deeper into the woods. She hoped she could find her way back since for some reason the dog refused to use the path.

"Mop, get your ass over here," she bellowed when she just missed him again. Not that she was getting annoyed. But she was.

Maybe her frustration penetrated his tiny little brain, because the next time she spotted him—in a clearing—he stood still, waiting for her to approach. Her steps slowed as she neared. Not because she wanted to sneak up on him, but because the clearing where he stood was…strange.

She couldn't put her finger on why it sent shivers up her spine, but it did. Though the trees surrounding it were large and dense, nothing grew here. The forest floor was dirt—not even ferns or mushrooms or moss. To her surprise, she realized there were what looked like ancient stones circling it. When she stepped between two of the pillars, a bolt of electricity shot through her. When she touched one, it happened again. She drew back and studied it, noting the markings on the face of the column. She didn't understand the symbols carved there, even though, as a historian, she'd studied hieroglyphics and cuneiform. These markings were unfamiliar. Rune-like, perhaps.

Very curious.

And fascinating.

Funny that she'd never found this place as a child, when they'd played in these woods, but maybe she'd never come this far before. She glanced at the sky, but it was blotted out by the canopy of trees. Still, she could tell it was getting dark. Too late to explore this interesting site, but she would come back tomorrow, if she could find it again.

"All right, you imp," she said, heading for Mop. "Let's go have some pizza." She tucked the flashlight into her pocket and scooped him up, but he yelped and wriggled from her grasp. To her complete and utter annoyance, he skittered away again.

She made a sound, a growl or a snarl or something like that, and started after him but at that moment, the clasp on her locket broke and it fell to the ground.

It was an old locket—no one really knew how old it was as it had been given to Grandma when she'd been a girl—but it was precious because Grandma had treasured it. And she'd given it to Maggie. She huffed a sigh and bent to pick it up.

Perhaps she bent too quickly, or perhaps she was weakened by lack of food—surely the pizza had arrived by now—but her head spun and she lost her balance and fell.

And fell.

And fell.

Barraged by a swirling welter of movement, blinded by flashing lights and stars flickering before her eyes, she tumbled. For some reason, the image of Alice plummeting into the rabbit hole flickered through her mind. She squeezed her eyes shut, tightened her hold on the locket and tried to focus on quieting her pattering pulse.

She'd never fainted before. Was that what this was?

How mortifying.

She landed with a thump, one reminiscent of waking with a jolt from a falling dream.

Sucking in a deep breath, she opened her eyes...and then closed them again as bright sunlight scored her corneas. What the—?

"What have we here?" A deep voice in a thick brogue echoed through the trees. Maggie sat up like a shot and scraped the hair from her eyes and stared at the man standing before her. He was tall and broad, with dark riotous curls and a fierce expression. He was dressed in strange clothes made of wool and had simple leather boots on his feet. He held a large bow with an arrow pointed at her heart.

Another man captured her attention. He was ferocious as well. In fact…they all were. No fewer than six rough and feral and thoroughly *unwashed* men surrounded her in a semi-circle.

It occurred to her that, though she was still in a circle of stones, they were not the same stones…and the forest was different. These trees were leafy where the ones at home had been firs. The angle of the light was off and the air…tasted different. She knew something very strange had happened, but her mind was having a hard time processing what it could have been.

Where was she? What had happened? Was this a hallucination? A dream? Had she died? Was this heaven? The men were certainly handsome enough for it to be.

And why was she still…tingling?

"What is it Declan?" One of the men asked.

The first man—the leader—looked her up and down. His lip curled and he sneered, "What is it? Why, a Cameron spy of course."

CHAPTER TWO

MAGGIE YELPED AS, WITHOUT WARNING, THE BURLY WARRIOR named Declan whipped her up into his arms and tossed her over his shoulder. To her dismay, she lost her hold on the locket and it fell into the thick grass.

"Wait," she cried. She wriggled to get free, but his grip was too hard. When she pummeled his back with her fists as he strode from the circle of stones, he chuckled. The beast. But to be fair, he was so large, it would have felt like a kitten batting him. "Put me down."

"I willna," he said. "The Macintosh will decide how you die."

All right. That shut her up. For a second. "Die? Why do I need to die?" What the hell had she ever done to him?

The man following, an enormous blond with a scar tracking his cheek, bent down to peer at her. "The Macintoshes doona tolerate spies."

"I'm not a spy." Seriously. She wriggled more and Declan smacked her ass.

Smacked her ass.

She'd kill him when she got free. Just kill him.

"Yer wearing the Cameron colors," the blond said in a growl. "And the Macintoshes doona —"

"Right. I know. The Macintoshes doona tolerate spies." Her head was starting to spin from being upside down and jounced around with each step. Her temper was on a short leash. "But honestly, if I were a spy, would I wear the Cameron colors? It seems a little counterproductive in my opinion. I mean, if I'm spying and all. I might as well wear a t-shirt that says, oh, I dunno, honk if you love spies."

His brow rumpled but he didn't respond. At least, not to her. "She speaks strangely," he complained to Declan.

Her captor snorted a laugh. "She dresses strangely too."

"Aye. She does at that. I've heard the Cameron lasses are a wild lot, but I had no idea —"

"I'm. Not. A. Cameron." She reached out and smacked the blond, but only because he came close enough. He reared back and gaped at her — as though he'd never been smacked before — and then he quickly moved out of range.

It hardly mattered, because, apparently, they had reached their destination, a camp on the edge of the woods. The sounds of nickering horses and clanks of pots gave her her first clue — she was facing the other way, after all.

Her second clue was that Declan dropped her on the ground. She landed with an oof. She glared at him. He didn't seem to mind in the slightest. "Go get my brother, Ewan," he barked, and the blond trotted off to one of the larger tents.

When she stood and brushed off her jeans, Declan bristled and she shot him a sardonic glare. Did he think she was stupid enough to run away? For one thing, these enormous men had her surrounded. For another, she never ran. Not if she could help it.

Instead, she made a quick survey of her surroundings. The camp was little more than a huddle of tents with the forest on one side and a sweeping plain on the other. A small herd of horses was hobbled to one side and a deer roasted over a pit fire. An entire deer. Before she could silence the thought—she often had that problem—she said, "You killed Bambi."

Declan's brow rumpled. "I dinna kill anyone." And then he asked, "Who is Bambi?"

"Never mind." She crossed her arms and turned away, pretending to ignore them. But she wasn't. She was aware they were all staring at her like she was a curiosity in a zoo, but she was taking in tiny details as well. Like the fact that their clothes were all handmade and simple. Their hair appeared to have been cut by Edward Scissorhands and most had beards, which were scraggly and long. But it was their weapons that really gave her pause.

One held a crossbow dating from the thirteenth century. Another had a Macintosh dirk that resembled one she'd seen in a museum. Declan had a simple calfskin sporran tied to his belt.

Odd. Could she have wandered into some Renaissance faire? But no, it had been evening when she stepped into the woods and now it was daytime. Early afternoon. And the forest surrounding Grandma's home went on for acres. It couldn't be—

"So." She flinched as a deep, melodious voice wafted to her on a ribbon of humor. Shivers danced through her, along with a prickling sense of premonition. "Ye have captured a Cameron spy?"

She turned slowly and froze as her gaze landed on him. On that so-familiar face. Broad, handsome, savage. Much more captivating than the sketch had been. Much more captivating by far.

She must be hallucinating. She had to be.

He was the hero of her dreams come to life.

Dominic Dundragon, Laird of the Macintosh clan.

Large, looming and in the flesh.

Her head went woozy. Her vision blurred. And then, for the first time in her life, she fainted. For real this time.

* * *

No one caught the girl when she fell. Dominic shot a glare around the circle and the lot of them winced. As well they should. "Where did you find her?"

"Sleeping in the ciorcal cloiche."

"Sleeping there?" An odd place to sleep. He tipped his head to the side and studied her. Her clothes were odd, made of materials he'd never seen, from the Cameron blue of her trews to the blousy tunic covered in flowers. Her shoes were strange as well, made of a hard black substance and peppered with holes. But nothing captured his attention as much as her face. She was beautiful. Her features were delicately hewn, her hair was jet back and her neck was slender and swanlike.

His gaze flicked downward and he swallowed heavily. Aye. Her face was captivating, but not nearly as stunning as her form. Though she dressed like a man, there was no denying she had the curves of a woman.

And what a woman. He'd never met the like. Never clapped eyes on a creature so bewildering and…alluring. Lust, and something, else rose within him. She was—

"You ye think she's a fairy?" Young Duncan piped up.

Snorts rounded the circle. They were all braw warriors. Not one of them believed in fairies. Probably.

"Nae," Ewan said. "More likely an elf."

Dominic glared at him. "She's no' an elf. She's a girl."

Ewan scrubbed at his beard. "She looks like an elf."

"More like a fairy," Tavish said.

"Bean-Nighe more like." This, from Harry.

Declan gave a growl. "She's no' Bean-Nighe, fairy nor elf. She's a spy." He turned to Dominic and glowered. "We should run her through."

Dominic didn't know why the prospect set up such a churn in his belly.

"Before we run her through, we should fook her."

He whirled on Tavish, who reared back at the ferocity of his scowl. Dominic had no idea why he scowled, but the prospect of this lot fooking her made him want to rip someone limb from limb. Possibly Tavish.

His cousin blinked. "Well?" He waved at the girl. "She is a comely lass."

"She's a spy," Declan spat.

Dominic attempted to calm his thudding pulse. "What makes you think she's a spy?"

"She's wearing the Cameron blue."

He scrubbed his face with a palm. "If she were a spy, do ye' think she would proclaim her loyalties so?" Would she be so conspicuous in it?

Ewan chuckled and shot a smirk at Declan. "That's what she said."

"No doubt that is what a spy would say, were she captured. We should run her through before she awakes."

"We're no' running her through."

Declan opened his mouth to protest, but Dominic cut him off with a slash of his hand.

"When she wakes up, we will question her. Try to discover who she is and what she's doing on our lands. What did she say when you asked her?"

A red tide crept up his brother's cheeks, confirming Dominic's suspicion. "I dinna ask."

"You dinna ask."

"Nae."

He turned to Ewan. "Take her to my tent and tie her securely. And Ewan?" he barked when his kinsman leaped forward to do his bidding, hauling the woman into his arms as though she were a ragdoll.

He paused and shot Dominic a curious glance. "Aye, laird?"

"Be gentle."

For God's sake. Be gentle.

* * *

When Maggie woke up, she was in a musty old tent. There was a rickety table and two chairs on the far side, but the bed was little more than a pallet, a pile of furs on the ground. It took a moment for her to remember what had happened. It took longer for her to accept it.

Even though she was here, living it, breathing it, it was inconceivable that she had traveled through time and space to him. As though drawn to him like filings to a magnet.

Or something.

She decided to try and be logical about it, or as logical as she could be. She sat up and looked around, taking stock of the period clothing tossed on a trunk, the weave of the tent material and the leather bindings that held it to the poles. There was no doubt she wasn't in Kansas anymore — or Seattle — but it was the fact that he was here that really made her head spin.

And gawd. He was even hotter in person.

She tried to brush her hair from her face and realized her wrists were tied, which was very annoying. But she wasn't sure which was more irksome — the fact that they'd tied her wrists together, or that they hadn't bothered to do a very good job of it. Apparently they thought her far too feeble to work the bonds loose, too stupid to use her teeth to untie the simple knot.

Once free, she stood and brushed herself off, then she crept to the flap and peered out. A boy stood by the fire, tending the roasting deer, but other than him, the camp was empty. Or at least, none of the other warriors were visible.

Excellent.

Sucking in a deep breath, she tiptoed from the tent and darted into the woods.

Though they'd hauled her here—kicking and screaming—she was pretty sure she could find her way back to the stone circle. Obviously it was some kind of portal—some wormhole in time, to use Jenny's description—that connected these two places in time-space. If she could get back to the circle, maybe she could get back home. To pizza. Not that she was starving...but she was. If nothing else, she wanted to rescue her locket before someone else found it.

She probably should have watched where she was going, rather than peering over her shoulder to make sure no one was following, because she slammed into a tree.

Wait. Not a tree. A wall.

No. Too warm to be a wall. It was...

Crap.

It was him.

His chest to be specific. He was so tall she had to tip back her head to see his face. He was not amused. Those perfectly-defined features were arranged into a frown.

"And where do ye think yer going?" His voice was low and melodious; it sent a skitter up her spine. Made something unnerving churn in her belly, heat rise on her neck.

She ignored all that and pulled herself from his grasp.

Apparently he didn't want to release her so it devolved into something of a scuffle. With a lurch, she reared back and stepped away because, seriously, she couldn't think with him that close. At least, not think logically. All she could focus on was the way he smelled—manly and musky—the heat rolling off him in waves, his piercing stare.

She swallowed her drool and crossed her arms and attempted to look him in the eye. "What, ah, what was the question?" Yeah. It was that bad.

"Where are ye going?"

"To hell if I don't change my ways."

The highlander reared back and stared at her as though he'd never heard a snarky response before. As though he'd not smelled so much as a whiff of insubordination. As though no one ever dared.

Well, she dared. She dared just fine.

She put her hands on her hips to make the point.

His brow lowered. "Where are ye going, lass?" This in a gentle tone that somehow brooked no defiance.

She waved her hand in some vague direction. "Back."

He tipped his head to the side and smiled. It was a sad smile limned with pity. It was also breathtakingly gorgeous. Dimples erupted on his cheek above his neatly-trimmed beard. "I doona think so."

"I most certainly am." She ripped her gaze from his face and focused on a tree, or a bush. Whatever. Just not on his face. His scent assailed her, fuzzing up her thinking process. Still, she was able to sputter, "I don't belong here."

"You realize we canna let you go." He said it so softly, in such a poignant tone, she glanced at him before she could stop herself. His eyes were gray, like a stormy day at sea, but they were calm and steady as he waited for his meaning to register.

"Of course you can let me go. You need to let me go. I have to get back—"

"Back where? To the Camerons?"

She gusted a melodramatic sigh. "I'm not a Cameron. I believe I mentioned that before." Several times.

"Then why are you wearing Cameron blue?"

She smacked her leg. "These are jeans. Everyone wears them where I come from."

"Aye. And the Camerons all wear blue."

"It's hardly the same thing."

"Is it no'?"

He opened the flap of the tent and she realized with surprise that he'd been leading her back to the camp. She hadn't even been aware of it. That, if anything, was evidence of how dangerous a man he was.

"Sit down." He nodded to a chair.

She didn't care for the thread of command in his tone, so she didn't comply.

His brow rumpled, as though one of his commands had never been so blatantly ignored. "Sit."

"You could say please."

He blinked. "Why would I say please?"

"Because it's polite."

"'Tis polite to offer a chair." His enormous shoulder lifted. "But if you prefer to stand, so be it." He settled himself into a chair and leaned back with a sigh. He folded his fingers over his middle and looked up at her, though he didn't have far to look. With him sitting, they were nearly at eye level.

Maggie frowned at him. And at the other chair. And at him again. And then she sat. Not because he commanded it. But because she wanted to sit. That was all.

His smile annoyed her, but at least he tried to hide it. He turned away and poured liquid into two flagons and set one before her.

She glared at it. "What's that?"

He took a deep draw on his. "Just water."

"Just water?" She picked up her cup and sniffed, then took a sip. Cool, fresh water bathed her throat. It was beyond delicious. Maggie didn't think she'd ever tasted anything like it. She emptied her cup and then held it out for more.

As he refilled her flagon, he studied her. "So, lass," he said. "What is your name?"

It seemed churlish not to respond. He had given her water after all. "Maggie Spencer."

He quirked a brow. "Maggie?"

"Margaret, really. But no one calls me that."

"Ah. You were named for the Maid."

"The Maid?"

"The Maid of Norway."

Oh. That Maid. Margaret had been the Queen of Scotland. "Sure." Whatever.

"And from where do you hail, Maggie Spencer?"

"Seattle."

"Seattle? I've not heard of this place."

"It's…east of here." Far east.

"East? But you were found to the south."

There was no response to that, so she decided to turn the topic. "And your name?" She was pretty sure, but a confirmation would be nice.

"I am Dominic Dundragon. Laird of the Macintosh Clan of Dar."

Even though she'd known, a shiver danced through her. She stared down into her cup. "Dominic is not a Scottish name."

"Nae." He chuckled. "It's from the Latin, Dominicus, meaning Of the Lord. I was born on a Sunday."

"I see."

"And now..." He leaned closer. His breath bathed her face. "Maggie of Seattle, why were you sleeping in the ciorcal cloiche?"

"The what?"

"The stone circle."

"I wasn't sleeping there."

He frowned. "All right. What were you doing there?"

Well hell. How to answer that? She could hardly tell him the truth. She didn't even believe the truth herself. And if she had somehow stepped into the thirteenth century, it probably wasn't wise to suggest she had magically traveled through time. It would be damn inconvenient if they burned her as a witch. "I was... lost."

"Lost?"

The thread of disbelief in his tone annoyed her. "Yes. Lost. Haven't you ever been lost before?"

"No. I canna say as I have."

That annoyed her too. He was far too condescending. She blew out a huff. "Yes, well, I got lost. Would you mind telling me where I am?"

"You're in Dar."

"Scotland?"

Her question took him aback. He stared at her for a long while before he answered. "Aye. Scotland."

His perusal made her uncomfortable. She shifted in her chair. Then she said the first thing that came into her mind, which, as always, was unfortunate. "I thought Dar was a castle."

His brows lowered. "Aye. Dar is the name of my home. My village. My lands. Clearly you know this of us at least." His sudden suspicion was palpable. "And how did you come by this knowledge, Maggie of Seattle? A woman who does not even know the name of the country she has wandered to the center of?"

She sniffed. "I read it in a book."

She was not prepared for his response. He reared back and gaped at her. "You...read?"

"Of course I read." Upon reflection, she should have remembered that few people were literate in this world. Most especially the women. "Everyone in Seattle can read." She shot him a look. "We're very progressive."

"I...see. And what was the name of this book?"

"The Macintoshes of Dar."

"A whole book dedicated to my clan?"

Oh dear. This wasn't helping. He was becoming even more leery. She decided to go all in. "It's my clan too." It was. Though she was 700 years removed. Everyone in her family had descended from one man, Liam Macintosh, the lone survivor of the Urquhart Ambush.

Dominic stilled. "You are a Macintosh?"

"Yes."

"The Macintoshes of Seattle?"

Um. Sure. "Yes."

"Why have I never heard of this sept?"

"I told you. We're from the west."

"I know all the clans to the west."

"We're from across the sea."

His eyes narrowed. "There is nothing across the sea."

"There is." Seattle, for one thing. Also, Vegas. But she didn't see the point in mentioning that.

He was silent for a long while. When he finally spoke, his voice was low and somber. "All right. Assuming you are, indeed a Macintosh from Seattle...why are you here?"

Oh crap. How the hell was she supposed to answer that? She didn't know. Not really. She decided to go with her gut. To give him the one answer that had been humming in her soul since she clapped eyes on his picture.

"I came to meet you, Dominic of Dar. I came to meet you."

CHAPTER THREE

SOMETHING WHIPPED THROUGH DOMINIC LIKE A HOWLING wind. He wasn't sure what it was, but it was hot and needy. Certainly, she was a strange little thing. Certainly her story was suspect. But he couldn't shake this sense of…recognition. The overwhelming sense of inevitability. As though the two of them were meant to meet. Meant to be together. Meant to —

And yes, his passion was high.

He wanted her with a hunger he had never known. He wanted to pull her into his arms and kiss her, ravage her, claim her.

But his brain overruled his hunger. It had to. He had hundreds of kinsmen beneath his banner and he was devoted to protecting them. He could not succumb to simple lust with a woman who could be a traitor. Who could be lying every time she parted those pretty lips.

But it wasn't simple lust, was it? There was nothing simple about it.

He sat back and studied her, but in truth, he needed a moment to rally his resolution, his sanity.

"You say you have come from Seattle to meet me?"

"Yes."

"Why?"

Her mouth opened. He fixated on it. He hardly even noticed the fact that she didn't actually respond, that a flicker of befuddlement crossed her face. Would she not know why she had come to meet him?

At length, she burbled, "Well, to meet the great Laird of Dar, of course. Everyone knows of you in Seattle."

Again, he had the sense her words were lies, but he didn't dwell on the suspicion. There seemed little point. All that mattered here, all that should matter, was keeping his people safe from their enemies. There had been many raids on his lands of late, many treacheries from the Cameron Clan to the east. Whispers of betrayal abounded, especially now, with the forming of the Chattan Confederation. The Camerons had not been included in the federation of clans and—resentful of the exclusion, or worried the combined forces of so many families would become too powerful— were determined to scuttle the union.

More than one Cameron spy had been captured, and many Cameron lads had come to Dar to cause mischief. They were becoming a familiar nuisance.

But they'd not yet sent a woman.

Though he was certain she was lying, he was also certain she wasn't a spy.

What she was, was a mystery.

One he was determined to unravel.

Declan pushed into his tent and when he saw Dominic and their prisoner enjoying a drink at the table, he glowered. He glowered a lot.

"You were supposed to wait for me before you interrogated her," he grumbled.

"I'm no' interrogating her. I just thought she might like something to drink…after her stroll."

"Her stroll?"

"Aye." Dominic gestured to the ropes on his pallet. "Apparently Ewan's knots were no' strong enough to hold her."

"You did tell him to be gentle." This Declan said with a hint of repugnance.

"Oh, did you?" Maggie asked. Her expression brightened. She fluttered her lashes. "That was nice."

"I dinna want him to hurt you. But I expected him to tie you securely at least."

"Oh, the ropes were very secure," she said with a solemn nod.

Again, a lie. Why it made him want to grin, he didn't know.

"Well, now that I am here, we can begin," Declan said. There were no more chairs, so he stood, looming over Maggie with his arms crossed. To her credit, she didn't seem intimidated in the slightest. "Who are you, wench?" he barked.

For some reason, she grinned. "You're the second person to call me that today." But she seemed disinclined to answer, which annoyed Declan heartily.

Dominic sucked in a deep breath. "Her name is Maggie Spencer, of Seattle—"

"Seattle?" Declan's brows beetled. "Never heard of it."

"It's to the west, across the sea."

"It's a lovely town." Maggie leaned forward. "We have flying fish."

Declan snorted an imprecation and she batted her lashes...again. It almost seemed as though she *enjoyed* riling him. Which, upon reflection, was not terribly wise. She was fearless. Or foolish. He wasn't sure which.

"She claims she was coming to visit...Dar and became lost. This is why she was sleeping in the *ciorcal cloiche*."

"Technically, I wasn't sleeping."

"What were you doing there then?" Declan snapped.

She lifted a shoulder. "Falling, I presume."

His brother's lips worked, as though he found her too confabulating for words. But then, Dominic did as well. He didn't understand half of what she said. Finally, Declan huffed, "Well, none of this changes anything. She's a Cameron—"

"I'm *not* a Cameron."

"She's a Macintosh." They both spoke at the same time.

Declan fixed his stare on Dominic. "A Macintosh? But why is she wearing blue?"

"Apparently everyone in Seattle wears blue."

"Everyone? Inconceivable."

"Well, not *everyone*." Apparently she felt the need to clarify. "Just lots of people. It's doesn't *mean* anything there. It's just blue."

Dominic shook his head, trying to make sense of this. "How can you tell which clan people are from?"

"You don't."

Both Declan and Dominic gaped. "You doona? How on earth did you know if you're with friend or foe?"

"In Seattle it doesn't matter. Everyone lives together in peace." She paused and thought about that for a moment, then added, "Well, almost everyone. God help you if you cut in line at Starbucks."

He had no idea what Starbucks was, but Seattle did, indeed, sound like a wonderful place, one where a man did not always have to be watching out for a dagger in the back.

But again, probably a lie.

Or a fantasy.

Maybe she was touched.

Oh, he didn't like that prospect in the slightest, but he did have to consider it.

After all, flying fish?

Maggie sighed. "I'm enjoying this interrogation and all, but would you mind so terribly much giving me something to eat while you barrage me with questions?"

"I'm hardly barraging you."

"I haven't eaten in hours. I'm starving."

She didn't look as though she was starving—far too many curves for that—but there was no denying the growl from the general region of her belly. Dominic nodded to Declan. "Bring her a slice of the venison."

Her nose wrinkled. "Bambi?"

Ironically, Declan's nose wrinkled too. "I doona want to leave you alone with her. She could be dangerous."

Dominic glanced at her, the tiny wee thing. He knew she had no weapons on her; Ewan had found nothing but a strange metal tube in her pocket when he'd checked for them. And she was...small. Delicate. Feminine. "She's no' dangerous."

"Oh, I'm very dangerous," she gusted. "I know jiu jitsu."

Declan shot her a frown, then turned it on Dominic. "I'm hardly a serving boy."

"I know that. But I would verra much appreciate it if you could bring our guest something to eat. Before she collapses again."

She set her hand on her stomach and arranged her features in a pleading moue. "I am *verra* hungry."

"Well, hell." Declan glared at both of them and stomped from the tent.

"My," Maggie said, staring after him. "He's grumpy."

Dominic tried not to chuckle. Declan was grumpy. Moody and dour. But he was one of the fiercest warriors Dominic knew, and he loved him very much. Enough to overlook his disposition. "You understand why he is suspicious of you, do you no'? You come to us wearing the colors of our enemies at a time when hostilities are high—"

"Hostilities were always high between the Macintoshes and the Camerons," she said.

Something prickled at his nape. "*Were?*"

"Um, always have been?"

He sat back and studied her, his mind awhirl. The Macintoshes and the Camerons had not always been at odds. The feud had begun only recently, with the convocation of the Chattan Clans. When Torquil Cameron had been excluded from the discussions. But he was an ornery bastard. Hot tempered and rash. "So you know of the disputes between our clans in Seattle? It is written in this book?"

She nodded.

"And what else does the book contain?"

A flush rose on her cheeks. "Well, lots of stuff."

"Such as?"

"History. The lines of kings. Lairds. Battles. I know that Dar came to the Macintoshes through William the Lion in 1155. The lands were expanded through an alliance with the Shaws in 1214. There was a kerfuffle in 1281 when King Alexander died and Clan MacBain tried to claim the land. And then in 1291—"

She broke off and glanced at him. Her flush deepened.

"In 1291?"

"Nothing." She shook her head. "Nothing. That's all I know."

He did not believe her. She knew more. She knew something. He leaned forward and pinned her with an intense look. "What happened in this year of our Lord?"

"This year?"

"Aye. 1291."

Her throat worked. "It's 1291?"

He shot her a dark glance and she shrugged.

"I've...lost track of time." A huffed and manic laugh. "Where does it go?"

"What happens?" A growl.

"Clan Chattan formed, of course."

No. There was something more. Something she was keeping from him. But he did not have a chance to probe deeper because Declan returned with a platter of venison, which he dropped before her with a clang.

She studied it askance. "Is this a lead plate?"

Declan narrowed his eyes. "'Tis pewter."

She sighed and picked up the meat between two fingers. "You really shouldn't use pewter," she said.

For someone who was *starving*, she nibbled at it rather gingerly.

He had to ask. Just had to. "Why should we no' use pewter?"

She rolled her eyes. "It's made with lead. Lead is poisonous."

He nearly laughed out loud. Cups and plates had been made from pewter for centuries. If lead were poisonous, they'd all be dead. Still, she ate the venison in tiny bites, meticulously avoiding the side that had touched the plate.

Declan watched, his hands on his hips, an expression of disgust on his face. "So," he said. "What do we do with her?"

Keep her. The thought rang in Dominic's head. *Keep her.* "We'll take her back to Castle Dar."

Declan's head whipped around. He frowned. "But we're no' done hunting."

"We have a good start."

"Not nearly enough for the winter." He glowered at Maggie, who shot him a cheerful grin as she licked her fingers. "We should stay a little longer."

A trickle of concern dribbled through him. Surely it was not fear he might lose her if he did not secure her in his keep? She'd already escaped once. No doubt she would try again. But Declan was right. Winter was coming and they needed to prepare for the long, cold months ahead. "A few more days then. But we'll be keeping you under guard." This he said to Maggie. Just so she knew they would be watching.

He disliked the thought of keeping her tied up, but disliked the thought of her slipping away even more. He didn't have the time or the inclination to explore the conundrum, because just then, Declan nodded and said, "We shall tie her to a tree for the night," and every thought flew from his head.

He bounded to his feet as annoyance and fury and something more whipped through him. "We are no' tying her to a tree." There was no need to bellow, the tent was small after all, but the roar was out before he could stop it. Surely he hadn't been entertaining the thought of keeping her here? With him? On his pallet? Wound together?

Surely he hadn't been entertaining other thoughts as well, there in the dark and shadowy recesses of his mind.

Guilt slithered through his gut.

All right, perhaps he had been. A little.

Declan crossed his arms. "I doona have time to build a cage for her."

Dominic gaped at him. His jaw dropped. "A cage?"

"She is a spy."

"She's a wee lass."

"I'm hardly a *lass*." He ignored the sniffed rebuttal from his side. "And I am hardly wee." She brushed down her thighs. "But thank you for saying that."

"We doona know who or what she is, Dominic. Think on it. Who knows what mischief she could cause?" Declan glowered at Maggie. She fluttered her lashes at him. "The Camerons are a murderous lot."

His ire rose, along with his voice. "We're no' locking her in a cage—"

"Excellent. Because I believe I mentioned I doona have time to build a bluidy cage—"

"She's staying here. With me."

Silence fell like an anvil. Declan stared at him. And, for that matter, so did Maggie. He hadn't intended for the words, the intention to escape, but it had. And now that it was said, he would not reverse his decision.

"Pardon me?"

He turned to her. Stared down at her beautiful face. Imagined lying next to her all night...and aching. He wouldn't get a wink of sleep. Maybe the tree was a better idea...

"Aye?"

She forced a smile, though he saw the wobble in it. "I can't help noticing...you have only one bed. Well, pallet, really. Where would I... Where would you..."

Oh, he liked this. He liked seeing her assurance crumble. Not that he didn't appreciate a confident woman, but this one was too confident by far. He didn't mind intimidating her a little. He didn't mind in the least.

He curled his lips into something of a smile. "Why, we shall sleep together, of course."

"What?" She and Declan squawked at the same time.

"'Tis the only way I can be sure you doona slip away into the night."

Because, by God, she would not escape from him again.

* * *

Oh good Lord. She wasn't going to sleep a wink and she knew it. For one thing, he was large and hogged most of

the bed. She couldn't even get comfortable because he'd
tied her hands — securely this time — and bound the rope to
the tent stake.

For another thing, he smelled.

Oh, not the stench one might expect of a man from the
thirteenth century without the benefit of body wash and a
steam shower. It was something tantalizing and evocative.
She couldn't put a name to it, other than the fact that he
smelled, quite simply, like a *man*. A man who worked hard
every day, who used his muscles and toned his body and
ate healthy food.

With each breath she drew it into her lungs, his essence,
his taste.

It was driving her crazy, making her dizzy and causing
unwanted thoughts to career through her mind.

Well, perhaps they weren't unwanted, but they were
certainly unwelcome.

She'd been attracted to this guy long before she'd met
him. She'd been half in love with the lines on his face.
Confronted by his person, the power of his presence, the
thrum of his energy, she found herself sliding quickly into
the mire of obsession.

His snore riffled through the room — it annoyed her that
he could sleep — and then he rolled over, toward her. His
heavy arm fell across her belly. She tried not to wince. He
pulled her closer, against him. His heat scorched her.

When he huffed out a sigh, his breath caressed her face.
Ah. God.

She could turn her head, just a little, and they would be
lip to lip. She could *taste* him.

The force of her desire startled her, and maybe
frightened her a little.

As attractive as he was, it wasn't wise for her to start
anything with him. Not in her situation. She was their

prisoner. His brother wanted her dead. Worse, if she made a slip and indicated how very not-from-here she was, it might be the end of her.

People from this century were not very open-minded about the prospect of time travel.

Or educated women. Who *knew* things.

Like the fact that at some point in the near future, he and most of his men would be murdered. And later in the fall, a flood would take out all their crops. Most of the clan would starve to death when the snows came.

1291 had been a banner year for the enemies of the Macintoshes.

It was a pity she couldn't warn him.

But even if she could—and he did not burn her at the stake—he wouldn't believe her.

Hell, *she* wouldn't believe her.

She stilled as his palm flattened over her belly...and then began to rove. He made a sound, something like a murmur. It rumbled through her ear. He edged closer, curling his body against hers. And shit.

That hardness against her thigh?

Unmistakable.

She nearly came out of her skin as his breath brushed her neck, and then his lips.

Jesus, God, they were warm and damp and sent skitters of delight through her body. Who would have suspected that such a simple touch could set her on fire? He opened his mouth and suckled her there and then his kiss walked up her neck to her lobe. A nibble there made her gasp. She tightened her hands into fists to keep from grabbing him— even though there was no fear of that, as they were locked above her head.

When his hand skated upward and cupped her breast, when his thumb scudded over her hard nipple, she moaned aloud.

He lifted his head. Their gazes clashed. He stared at her for a long moment, motionless and silent. Though his thumb did continue a tormenting scrape over her swelling nub.

A message passed between them. She was not sure what it was or what it meant, but something in her shifted. It was as though a curtain had been drawn away.

She didn't know why she'd been brought here, but she was a firm believer in destiny. Deep in her heart, she believed she'd been brought here—for whatever reason—to meet *him*.

And she wanted him. With more passion and ferocity and anguish than she'd ever felt for any man.

It would be a sin not to take advantage of this opportunity to finally taste him.

She would never forgive herself if she missed out.

So when his head descended, and his mouth neared hers…she didn't turn away. She met her destiny head on.

CHAPTER FOUR

SHE WAS SWEET, SO SWEET. HER MOUTH WAS FRESH AND SHE tasted like spring. Beyond that, she shocked him with her response to his kiss. She rose up to it. Met it. Matched him kiss for kiss.

He'd been caught unawares, having fallen asleep and dreamed of her, and then awoken to find her in his arms, warm against him. His desire had been riding high and he was only incited to further madness by her scent, her curves, her murmurs.

He wanted her. Wanted to take her here and now.

Something within him, some maddened beast, demanded he do just that. She was his prisoner. He had the right.

Another voice, one of irritating reason, argued against such folly. And not just because she was possibly an enemy trying to cozen him and seduce him, and weaken his guard against her—though there was that. But because he did not want to take her against her will. While she was bound and helpless.

Something deep within him railed at the prospect. He wanted her warm and willing in his arms.

Although she did not seem unwilling.

Ah, that was a dangerous thought, was it not?

She arched up into his kiss, nudging her tongue between his lips and his thoughts flew.

Good Christ. Where had she learned to kiss like this? The query threatened to gut him but he decided to ignore it and simply enjoy.

He explored her mouth, her chin, her neck—she really seemed to enjoy that. His hold on her breast never wavered, because it was far too delightful to release. She was perfectly proportioned, sensual and woefully overdressed. He worked at the buttons of her tunic. They were impossibly small, but he managed to get them open, even though she attempted to distract him with maddened kisses to his neck.

When he separated the placket and gazed down at her breasts, he blinked. She wore another garment, one that covered her in a band. Though he tugged it this way and that, he could not figure out how to remove it. If this was some kind of Cameron chastity belt, it was truly heinous.

"The hook is in the back," she gusted in a breathless voice. She leaned to the side, but in the shadows he could not see what he was doing and the odious contraption would not come undone.

She wailed in frustration at his fumbling attempts. "Untie me. I'll do it."

Dominic stilled. Disappointment flickered through him. It was foolish of him to assume her passion was true. It was an old gambit of captured women, to seduce a man to the point he loses all reason and then lure him into lowering his defenses. Dominic would not be had. "I canna untie you, lass."

She rolled back over and glared at him. "Why? Are you into some kind of Fifty Shades thing?"

His brow rippled. "I doona understand the meaning of this Fifty Shades thing."

"Yeah, well nobody does. Not really. Just untie my hands."

"I canna untie you."

She blew out a breath. "You can tie me back up once I take off my bra. Okay, Mr. Grey?"

Who?

But he didn't ask. He studied her. Though she seemed sincere, he could not slough off the fact that she'd not been completely honest with him. He knew it to the core of his being. He could not take the chance of untying her, even for this.

Even for the glory this might become.

He shook his head. "Nae."

She growled — something ferocious that sounded like "fine" — and with great effort rolled away from him. He felt a hint of guilt then, at keeping her tied, making her so uncomfortable, but it was consumed by the fire of his passion that, now inflamed, would not recede.

He lay back, closed his eyes and tried not to think of her taste, her scent, the curve of her breast.

He tried not to dream of her.

He failed.

* * *

Maggie woke up alone, but wrapped in a warm cocoon. It occurred to her that at some point, the highlander had woken up, untied her and left.

She tried not to let disappointment ripple through her at the fact he hadn't tried once more to remove her bra. Hell, that he hadn't kissed her again.

The kiss still danced in her mind. She swore she could still taste him.

She sat up and glanced around the tent. She was gratified to see a flagon of water and something on a plate on the table. She extricated herself from the furs and padded over to see that it was. Her nose wrinkled. An oat cake. She picked it up and nibbled at the corner. It wasn't terrible, but it wasn't orgasmic either. At the very least, it stopped the rumbling in her stomach.

If she kept eating like this, she might lose Survivor kind of weight.

She pushed her hair out of her face — without her brush she probably looked like a Chupacabra — and peered out the flap of the tent. Other than a few murmured conversations the camp was quiet, but she wasn't a fool.

The Macintosh would not have untied her unless he was certain she couldn't run. She glanced at the woods and had a momentary urge to flee, but pushed it away with a sigh.

Fact was, she didn't want to leave him. Not really. After that kiss, she wanted only one thing.

More.

Whatever this was, this adventure — or hallucination — she owed it to herself to explore it. Her only regret was that she really wanted her locket back. It meant the world to her.

She sighed and stepped out of the tent. A sudden movement at her side captured her attention and she glanced over as the large Viking-like man — the blond she'd smacked yesterday — leaped to his feet. He'd been sitting on a stool by the tent, whittling a stick down to a nub.

She forced a smile. "Good morning," she chirped.

He frowned at her, clearly put out by her affability. But then, he offered a begrudging nod.

"What are you doing?" she asked, gesturing to his stick.

He held it up and touched the pointy end with a finger. "Spear."

Ah. It was charming the way he responded with one word answers so she could understand him, being a *woman* as she was. "I thought you forged steel tips for your spears."

He gaped at her. "I...aye. But I was bored. And curious."

"Curious about what?"

"If this would be effective."

"No doubt it would be. It is very sharp."

"It is." You'd think she'd complimented his sexual prowess, the way he grinned.

"But short."

His glee deflated.

"You'd have a hard time getting close enough to get a good bead on your prey."

"Bead?"

"Good aim."

He studied the stick. "Aye. I think you're right."

"But you could lash it to a longer stick."

"Aye." He cast around for a longer stick.

"You're Ewan, aren't you?" She thought she remembered his name, but she wasn't sure. He nodded. "And how did you get guard duty, Ewan?" she asked in a teasing tone.

A flush rose on his cheeks. He mumbled something.

She tipped her head to the side and waited.

"I doona have the best...bead."

She blinked. "I beg your pardon?"

"The best aim. The others have gone hunting and I was chosen to stay behind because my aim is poor. I always undershoot."

"Ah. You need to aim for where it's going to be, not where it is." Yeah. Great advice. She'd learned that from a sage old man…in a movie. Too bad she couldn't remember which one.

His eyes widened. He stared at her. "Aye. Aye. I see what you mean." His face broke into a grin.

Well fricking finally. Finally one of them was smiling at her. It was a breakthrough of monumental proportions…until Declan stormed through the trees and glared at Ewan.

"What are you doing?" he barked.

Poor Ewan blushed again. "We were just talking."

"Don't talk to her. She's the enemy." He glared at her wrists. "How did you get untied?"

Annoyance prickled her, which was probably why she fluttered her lashes and cooed. "You have to ask your boss."

"My what?"

"Your laird. Apparently he felt I didn't need to be chained like a dog."

"I left Ewan to guard her." A deep voice, threaded with irritation, rode to her on the skeins of the air. Her head snapped in his direction. Her breath caught at his magnificence as he strode toward her. Good God. She hadn't imagined anything last night. He was the epitome of the Alpha male. "And I knew we wouldna be gone long." He turned to her; his features were taught, but there was a glimmer in his eye as he surveyed her. "Did you sleep well?"

"No."

His lips quirked up in a smirk only she could interpret.

"And I have to widdle."

He blinked. "What?"

"I need to use the ladies room."

The men exchanged confused looks.

She sighed. "I need to take a piss."

"Oh." They all lurched back as though she'd just announced she'd like to have some maggots for breakfast, thank you very much. Then the befuddled looks returned. Apparently none of them had considered the prospect that their prisoner might have the natural human need to evacuate her bladder at some point.

"I can go in the woods."

Dominic's expression darkened. "Not alone."

"I'm not peeing with an audience!"

"You're no' going alone." He rubbed his lips as he thought. And damn, they were fine lips. "I was going to the loch to wash up after the hunt. I'll take you with me."

The loch? It sounded lovely.

"I'll need to tie you up again, of course."

And yeah, her mood dropped.

He did. He did tie her up, although it was a loose configuration around her waist. And though he led her through the woods on a leash, she didn't mind so terribly because he talked her as they went. When she asked about an unfamiliar bird in the trees, he named it and pointed out others, and then when she asked about the hunt, he told her about that, and its importance to his people.

She listened and asked questions but tried not to share her own observations, because jabbering on as she had a tendency to do, she might share something disastrous. It almost felt like they had some kind of rapport by the time they came to the loch.

She was filled with visions of a nice soak in the sparking waters of the loch, of scrubbing her hair and washing off the sweat of the past two days, but when she saw it, her anticipation died a slow death.

It was not a loch so much as a muddy pond. She propped her hands on her hips. "That's the loch?"

"Aye." He bent down and began washing his hands in the water. He glanced up at her. "Did you need to…widdle?"

Oh, hell. Yes she did. She glanced around the clearing searching for a good spot.

He gestured to a bush. "There."

Her nostrils flared. "You'll be able to *see* me."

"The point."

She glared at him and stomped over to the bush, noting her leash was just barely long enough. Turning her back to him, she yanked down her jeans and, squatted and — good gravy, it felt good to Release the Kraken. But then she winced as she realized… she was peeing in the woods.

"Is there any toilet paper?" she asked, although it was a foolish question. "I mean something to wipe with?"

He tipped his head to the side and studied her as though she were an animal in the zoo. He ripped a bunch of leaves from a branch and handed them to her without a word.

Leaves.

She squeezed her eyes shut and did what she had to do. But honestly, in that moment, she didn't like the thirteenth century in the least.

* * *

She was a funny thing.

So confident and intelligent, but at the same time, so utterly clueless, as though she really did not belong in this place, in this world whatsoever.

As a child Dominic had been told stories about the fairies who visited from another realm to cause mischief, steal babies and occasionally mate with the human folk. If he'd had a whimsical bone in his body, he could have believed she was one of them.

But she was no fairy.

She was flesh and bone.

Human.

It had killed him watching her tug down her breeks, exposing her long legs and that delicious ass. He wanted to see her whole body, bare before him. Writhing.

If he had any sense, tonight he would strip her naked *before* he tied her up.

And hell.

What hell that thought unleashed in his gut.

She stood and fastened her pants — much to his regret — and then turned to face him. He tried to conceal his thoughts from her, but probably failed, because her eyes widened. Memories of the night before, holding her, kissing her, testing the exquisite weight of her breasts, howled through him. Her lips parted. Her tongue peeped out and hunger boiled.

Slowly, they approached each other, step by step.

He reached up and tucked a wild curl behind her ear. Lord she was lovely. Her eyes were clear, her complexion flawless. Her expression welcoming.

He bent his head, savoring the moment, savoring the anticipation of tasting her again.

A growl behind him made his heart stop

The little hairs of his neck stood on end.

He ripped his gaze from hers and whirled, keeping her behind him, shielding her from this menace.

An enormous, scarred beast stood in the shadows of the trees, its teeth bared, saliva dripping from its maw. A wolf.

Shite.

What had he been thinking, coming out into these woods alone? That he might steal a kiss?

Fool.

Wolves were a constant danger to hunting parties; the scent of blood drew them.

And Dominic had left his weapons in camp. All he had on him was a dirk.

Fear flickered in his breast. Not for himself. For her.

He at least had a chance.

She was utterly helpless before such savagery.

"Stay back," he murmured softly, positioning himself to meet this threat. The woman did not obey him. She crept along behind him, clutching his arm. He pulled out his dirk and waved his arms wide to make himself look bigger.

The wolf was not impressed. It padded closer and closer still, licking its chops. It growled again.

"Be careful," she said.

He dared an incredulous glance at her. *Be careful?* "Stay back," he snapped. "I want you to run when I attack."

"You're going to *attack*? That's a wolf. And a big one too."

"What would you have me do?"

"Throw it a chunk of meat."

"In case you havena noticed, the only meat I have is still attached to my body."

"Well you can't attack it—"

But he didn't have to. The wolf did the honors, leaping at him with a blood-chilling snarl.

They met in a macabre embrace. The force of the lunge knocked him to the ground. Sharp claws gouged at his leather jerkin and jagged teeth sprayed drool across his face as they snapped in a frenzy. It took all Dominic's strength to hold it back. The only thought in his head was that he had to prevail... or she would die.

He could not allow that.

He could not let his failure be the cause of her destruction.

But it was clear. He was outmatched. His only hope was to take a swipe at the beast with his knife and hope he hit some vital spot. Trouble was, he needed both hands to hold it off. He tried to roll over, to pin the creature beneath him, but it weighed more than he did, and had all the leverage.

Slowly, but surely, the gaping maw closed in, near and nearer to his jugular.

A horrendous roar resounded through the clearing. Something that sounded like "Hii-ya!" and the wolf went flying sideways into the dirt. It rolled and then leaped to its feet again, but its attention was not on Dominic. It was on Maggie.

And it was really angry now.

"I told you to stay back," he snapped.

"You were losing."

"I wasna losing."

She sniffed and muttered, "Were too."

The wolf lunged again, straight at Maggie. Horror clutched at his chest, locked his throat, screamed in his veins.

To his astonishment she held still before this oncoming monster and then, at the last second, stepped to the side, slamming the butt of her palm into the wolf's face.

It yelped, but whirled around to attack again. This time she hunched down and rolled to the side, landing another blow to the beast's belly as he passed.

It occurred to Dominic that he was standing there gaping, which was not a very manly thing to do, so he leaped into the fray. Between the two of them they fended off another attack. The wolf, now panting, narrowed its eyes on them, contemplating the next incursion, but apparently it decided it had had enough.

It turned around and limped back into the woods.

His breath came in harsh gasps. His pulse raced. Sweat beaded his brow.

They'd nearly died. *She'd* nearly died.

"Oh my God." Maggie stared after it, her mouth agape. Her breath was ragged, her color high.

"You were wonderful," Dominic said, pulling her into his arms and kissing her soundly. It was a celebratory kiss, and quick, but it wasn't near enough.

Her eyes glimmered with a fevered excitement. "Was that a wolf? Did we just fight off a wolf?"

"Aye." He wrapped his arm around her shoulder and tugged her back in the direction of camp, keeping an eye on the woods. The creature could come back and he didn't want to be caught unawares.

"A wolf. An honest to God wolf."

Her astonishment puzzled him. Wolves were common in Scotland; they plagued hunters and farmers alike. "Do they no' have wolves in Seattle?"

She snorted a laugh, a giddy thing, as though impelled purely by the effects of her fear. "Well, yes. We do. But only in the zoo. And wolves have been extinct in Scotland since—" She trailed off and shot him one of those chagrined looks he was becoming so familiar with.

Something rippled through his gut. Something very uncomfortable. "Extinct?" What the hell did she mean by that?

"Never mind," she said, tugging on his hand. "We should get back. It's not safe here."

But he would not allow her to distract him so easily. He picked up the pace and said, "Why would you say wolves are extinct in Scotland, Maggie?"

"I didn't say that."

"You did."

"You must have misheard me."

"I dinna. Why did you say that?"

She stopped short. The woman who was in such a hurry to reach the safety of the camp, stopped. Her expression was solemn. "Trust me Dominic, you don't want to know." And then she whirled on her heel and hurried down the track.

But he did want to know.

He did.

And he wanted to know where she'd learned to fight like a warrior. With no weapons but those God gave her.

CHAPTER FIVE

WHEN THE OTHER HIGHLANDERS HEARD THERE WAS A WOLF IN the woods, of course they all had to go hunt it.

Men.

But it left Maggie and Dominic alone in the camp, which she appreciated greatly. They walked back to his tent and she collapsed into a chair.

A wolf. A freaking wolf.

She'd never been so frightened, watching it inch closer and closer to Dominic's handsome face. She'd never been so afraid. Or so angry. Or so aroused. Adrenaline still surged through her veins. She'd heard the term blood lust before, but she'd never actually experienced it before.

She really wanted to go pummel something right now…

"Here." Dominic thrust something beneath her nose. A tumbler of amber liquid.

"What is it?"

"Whisky."

She wrinkled her nose. "I don't drink."

"Drink it. You've had a shock."

"So I should do shots?"

His brow rumpled. He dropped into the chair next to her and shook his head. "I doona understand most of the things you say, Maggie Spencer."

She shrugged and took the drink. "That's okay. It's mostly sarcasm."

He nodded. "Like that. There. No idea what it means."

"Trust me. It's pithy and clever."

"You *are* clever." His gaze was far too warm. "You saved us both today."

"*You* saved us," she said, patting his hand, because a man liked to feel manly. And he had fought well. It was cute how he flushed.

"Where did you learn to fight like that?"

She took a sip of the drink and liked the warm burn in her throat, so she took another. "Gym class."

He nodded, though it was clear, once again, that he didn't understand. But then, how could he? They were worlds apart.

"What did you mean when you said wolves have been extinct in Scotland?"

She choked on her drink. It took a moment to wheeze it out. He waited. "I...you... You misheard me." Lame. So lame.

"I dinna. And we both know it. Why do you no' want to tell me what you meant?"

Well hell. Maybe it was the wounded expression on his face, or the whisky or the aftereffects of their encounter with the gaping maw of death, but she just lost all her reserve. It whistled out of her like a deflating balloon. "I don't want to tell you, because if I do, you won't believe me."

"Why do you think I willna believe you?"

"Because it's a crazy story. And you already don't trust me. Besides, I don't quite believe it myself."

"But…"

She set her fingers on his lips. "Please, Dominic. Don't ask."

He stared at her, his gaze intent. The muscle in his cheek worked. And then he nodded. "All right." He spoke against her fingers, practically a kiss. "I willna ask. But one day you'll tell me, Maggie." She tried not to grin at the intimation there might be a *one day*.

And then she did grin, because he leaned in and kissed her.

And her wrists were not tied.

And there was no one to interrupt them.

And her passion was high.

And so, apparently, was his.

* * *

He couldn't resist, even if he'd wanted to.

She was far too alluring. Beautiful, brave, smart and fierce. And he'd been aching for her since last night. Since he'd tasted her. He deepened the kiss and a flicker of excitement whipped through his gut when she responded in kind. She was a woman who knew what she wanted and was not afraid to take it. He liked that about her. Liked it very much. Especially when she threaded her fingers through his hair and tugged, just a little. The gesture made clear her hunger was as raw as his, as undeniable. As feral.

When her tongue dabbed at his lips, pressed in, his head went light. His blood surged. His cock swelled. He launched to his feet, pulling her with him. He intended it to be a gentle move, but it was not. It was harsh and hungry, but she didn't seem to mind. She murmured something against his lips, something that might have been *Yes*.

He whipped her into his arms and carried her over to the pallet on the floor. He was certain she could have walked the short distance, but he was far too anxious. He didn't stop kissing her as he laid her down, but then, she didn't let him. Her hands were busy, tugging at his tunic, as he worked the infernal buttons of hers.

In the end, they got in each other's way and had to undress themselves.

With quick, short, desperate moves, he yanked off his tunic and breeks. It took her a bit longer to divest herself of her clothing, but he didn't mind. He enjoyed the show.

When the band encasing her breasts dropped away, he stilled. The breath locked in his lungs. Lord above, she was beautiful. Her scent—an undeniable arousal, tangled with something earthy and sweet—rose to meet him.

She opened her arms to him and he came to her. No force on earth could have stopped him.

He settled over her—glorying in the sleekness of her skin, of the sensation of her soft body pressing up into his hardness—and cupped her breasts, molded them, tasted them. He couldn't resist the coral target that possessed his attention. As his lips closed on her thrusting nipple, she moaned, wriggled. She was delicious. Delight danced through him.

As he sank into his explorations, her hands roved as well, over his chest, his belly. The noises she made incited him to madness—moans and sighs and wordless grunted commands. She wrapped herself around him, pulling him deeper into the kiss and raking his back with her nails.

Oh, Lord. Give me strength.

He had intended to prepare her, to launch a slow, sweet seduction. But such restraint was beyond him. Something about her incited a need that bordered on feral. A need to claim her, have her.

He did, however, take a moment to test her, to stroke her cleft. He loved that she spread her legs for him, without a word of request. He loved that her breath came in pants, that her eyes were wild, and her body quivered with need. She shuddered as his fingers scraped over the thick bundle of nerves nested at her core. To his utter gratification, it was slick. He ventured deeper, slipped down and in and— Holy heaven.

She was ready. So ready.

And tight.

Every muscle clenched. His gaze snapped to hers. Burned into hers. "Maggie…" A harsh growl. A snarl.

"Yes." She wrapped his hair in her fist and yanked; his hunger spiraled out of control. "Yes."

He fisted his cock and nudged her entrance. Her thighs widened. She stared at him, eyes wide, nostrils flared. Lips moving in a chant. *"Yes. Yes. Yes."*

He thrust, hard and deep.

She wailed her pleasure and arched her hips up, inviting him deeper still.

She was delicious. Delightful. Perfect. She held him hard and fast with the muscles of her sheath, clinging to him with a damp heat. His mind whirled, his chest locked. It was beyond perfect. It was heaven.

But need clawed. He pulled out—though it was torturous to do so—he pulled out and then lunged again.

And again.

And again.

She went wild beneath him, a she-wolf, snarling and raging and nipping at this skin in her frenzy. "Yes, Deeper. Harder."

He could not deny her. Indeed, he did not want to.

He cupped her ass in his palms and lifted her and, using her body as leverage, launched into a barrage of manic thrusts. From this direction and that, exploring her, invading her, possessing her completely.

Her head whipped from side to side. She writhed beneath him, closed her thighs on his hips. Her body tightened.

A quiver began deep in her core. It walked through his cock, through his body as well to settle in the base of his solar plexus. Rivulets of delight trickled through him, pooled, swelled.

He felt her tension mount and it enflamed his. His vision, his consciousness, his world closed in on one thing. The place where they joined, the heavenly connection where they were one.

His plunges became short and hard, desperate and crazed. He knew she was close but he could not, would not release until she'd found her bliss. He would hold back until that moment. He would wait for her. But it cost him. Sweat beaded on his brow. His heart hammered. His breath locked.

Please. Please. Please…

She released. It was not a peaceful surrender. She was passionate and powerful in her crisis. Her hold on him was fierce, her mouth hot as she roved over his shoulders, licking, nibbling and nipping with a mindless zeal.

And her hold on him… That tight grip on his wet and weeping cock. It made his vision blur, made his mind lock. Made his body fold in on itself.

In an agonizing, blinding rush of ecstasy, he erupted, flooding her with his seed, soaking her with his essence.

Though he was utterly drained, he continued to move, prolonging the pleasure for them both, though his thrusts were slow, easy, soothing.

All the while, he held her gaze, studying her, soaking her in. He loved that her lips quirked up, that she rose up to press her open mouth against his.

He eased her down into the furs and kissed her deeply. Her palms scudded over his back, exploring the gouges she had no doubt left there. "Mmm."

A murmur. His or hers. He wasn't sure.

He shifted to the side, though he hated withdrawing from her, and pulled her into his arms.

"I am verra sorry," he said, although it was probably a lie.

She stared up at him. Tucked his hair behind his ear. "Sorry? For what?"

"I dinna mean to ravage you."

Her laugh was something of a snort. "Was that what that was?"

"Aye." He'd been no better than a beast. Or at least, as good as one.

She put out a lip. "And here I thought I was ravaging you."

With no warning, a laugh rose up within him and he barked it out.

"Do you not feel ravaged?" This she said with a score of nails along his chest that sent a shiver of fresh arousal through him.

He grabbed her wrist in a tight cuff. Not that he didn't enjoy the sensation of being raked by her, but because he was certain he could not perform for her again...at least not for a long while. She'd devastated him. "A man ravages a woman. Not the other way around."

"Well, where I come from, men and women are equal. They can ravage each other."

He liked the idea. Liked it a lot. But he had to ask, "Did I hurt you?"

Her grin was wicked. "Did I hurt you?"

He turned to the side to show her his back. "I doona know. Am I bleeding?"

She kissed him there. Stroked him. "Only a little." He heard the smile in her voice. "You'll live."

He rolled back over and captured her in his arms and kissed her again with ferocity that matched his mood. "You were amazing." It needed to be said.

"So were you."

Their gazes locked and something deep inside him shifted. Solidified.

He didn't know who she really was, or where she came from or why she was here, but one thing was certain. He wasn't letting her go.

"You're mine now, Maggie." He said in a growl. No other man would have her. Not while he was alive.

* * *

You're mine now, Maggie.

The words resonated through her. Never before had she felt so complete, so wanted, so utterly...taken. He made love like a beast in heat and he spurred the same madness in her. Her body still hummed with pleasure, her mind still reeled.

She tucked herself into his embrace and gloried in the way he closed his hold on her. Their skin was sealed from groin to chest. Their heat mingled. Breath tangled.

His scent, his presence, sank into her, infusing her with an unutterable peace.

Perhaps she was being foolish to feel as though she had been brought here for this. As though the attraction, the draw between them had been strong enough to whisk her through time and space to his side, but the certainty roiling within her could not be denied.

"Promise me you willna leave," he murmured against her hair. "Promise you will never leave."

How could she promise? She had no idea how she'd come to be here. She had no idea how long she would stay.

She lifted her gaze to meet his. "I will never leave you," she whispered. But she had to add, to herself *Not of my own accord.*

It had to be enough. It was all she had.

It seemed to please him. His taut expression softened and he smiled—a brilliant explosion of joy and relief—and then he kissed her again.

The kiss threatened to swell into something more. His cock stirred against her thigh. He made a sound, a bestial rumble and shifted over her again. Her excitement flared.

Yes, he'd just brought her to the most mind-boggling fulfilment, but she was more than ready for another go—

"Oh hell." A harsh voice shattered their cocoon.

Maggie glanced over Dominic's shoulder and winced.

Honestly. Declan had the worst timing.

He stood in the door of the tent, holding the flap open. Behind him, all the others peered in, taking in the intimate scene.

Thank God her nakedness was shielded behind Dominic's big body—all his men could really see was his bare ass and her heated cheeks. He muttered something and tugged one of the furs around her and then he rolled off.

"Get out," he boomed.

Declan let the flap drop, but he remained inside the tent. He fixed a glower on his brother. "Tell me you dinna fook her."

Dominic snorted and stood, snatching up his breeks and tugging them on. He didn't bother with his tunic, for which Maggie was thankful. Because he truly was magnificent to look at. The sight nearly made her forget her own mortification.

"It's none of your business who I fook."

"Isn't it?" Declan glared at her. "She's a Cameron."

"Is she? She swears she is not and I believe her."

"Holy Christ, Dominic. How can you be so blind?"

"How can you?"

"She's using you. She's a siren, calling you to crash on the rocks with an enchanting song."

"Actually I'm tone deaf."

They both whipped around to stare at her and she rearranged her coverings and sat. She swiped her hair from her face.

"I can't sing at all. Seriously. Dogs howl."

Declan's fingers closed into fists. He appeared to be grinding his teeth. "It was a metaphor."

She shot him a sweet smile. "I know what it was."

"You are a vexing witch."

She didn't mean to wince at his words, but she did. Because that was the core of her fears. That they might think her a witch.

"She's no' a witch." Her heart thudded at Dominic's fierce defense of her.

"Has she no' bewitched you?"

"Nae. She hasna."

"Look at you. First chance you have and you're mounting her."

Dominic's eyes narrowed. "Hardly the first chance."

"That's true. He hardly touched me at all last night."

Declan gaped at her, sputtering his consternation. He whirled on his brother. "I ask you, nae, I beg you. Show some restraint. Until we discover who and what she really is, you must assume she is our enemy."

"She is no' our enemy. I know it. In my heart." He thumped his chest.

Declan reared back and stared at his brother, taking in the tautness of his features, the bunch of his muscles, his conviction. "And if she is? If she betrays us?"

Maggie didn't realize she was holding her breath, awaiting Dominic's response until her lungs started to ache. But still, she could not move, could not relax. Not until he glanced at her, his eyes glimmering. He held out his hand and took hers in it. Squeezed.

"She willna betray us, will you Maggie-mine?"

Maggie-mine. God. Her heart flipped over several times at those words, at his deep, steady tone.

She stared back at him, her soul in her eyes. "Nae," she said, unconsciously mirroring his brogue. "I willna. I will never betray you."

With a growl, Declan spun on his heel and ducked out of the tent, but he poked his head back in and snapped, "Oh, and in case you were wondering why I invaded your little love nest to begin with, Liam has arrived. There is news from Dar."

She had no idea why this announcement made Dominic snap to attention, why it made his expression darken. He merely nodded to his brother, who, with one more disdainful glance at her, quit the shelter.

Dominic blew out a breath and scrubbed his face. Then he bent and collected her clothing. "You should get dressed," he said. "If Liam has come all the way from Dar, the news must be important."

Apparently their tryst was over.

But then, Declan had completely spoiled the mood.

Maggie dressed quickly and then took Dominic's extended hand; he lifted her easily to her feet. He met her gaze and then pulled her into his arms again for another kiss. Though it was quick and far too brief, it was intense.

"You did promise no' to leave," he said.

She quirked a brow, unsure of his meaning. "I did."

"Good." Another kiss. "I really doona want to have to tie you up."

"Well, that's a relief," she quipped. "Because I really don't want to be tied up."

With a grin he took her arm and led her out of the tent to the fire where the other men were waiting.

A tall, sandy haired stranger stood among them. A strange shiver shot through her as she studied him. She'd certainly never met him before, but there was a familiarity about him she could not deny. He turned to her and their gazes clashed and the certainty grew.

"Liam," Dominic called, and greeted his vassal with a manly hug.

"My laird." He nodded to Maggie. "And who is this bonny lass?"

"Maggie Spencer, of Seattle. A visitor from our clansmen to the west. Maggie, this is my cousin Liam MacBain."

And suddenly, it hit her. Why he seemed so familiar. He looked much like the portrait of her grandfather's grandfather hanging in the library of their home. Same hair, same eyes, same hard sculpted chin. He was Liam MacBain Macintosh.

Her ancestor.

The man from whom her entire family had sprung.

CHAPTER SIX

Liam brought important news indeed.

After they had finished with the greetings and catching up of minor news from Dar, he asked to speak with Dominic and Declan in private. Dominic did not like leaving Maggie unattended, but he had words with Ewan — exhorting him to see her fed and, more importantly, to keep her safe. Not that he thought she'd run. She had promised she would not.

Beyond that, he knew all his men would watch over her. After what they'd witnessed in his tent, by now they all knew damn well she was his. But still, he hated being separated from her, even for a moment.

He led Liam to his tent as Declan brought in another chair and they sat around the table. Dominic poured them each a whiskey.

"So, what is the important news, Liam?" he asked.

His cousin took a swig of whisky and wiped his mouth with the back of his hand. "Verra good news, my laird. The MacPherson has agreed to your meeting. In fact, he has called for a convocation of the lairds to discuss concessions."

That was good news. Macpherson had been the only clan chief resisting the formation of a Clan Chattan federation. Dominic had been trying to arrange a meeting to confer with MacPherson over the matter, but he'd been obstreperous.

"Aye. They've all agreed to meet the day after tomorrow at Urquhart Castle."

Dominic's brow wrinkled. An odd place for a convocation, though upon reflection, it was neutral territory. None of the rival clans could claim superiority because it belonged to the Black Comyn, who had no stake in this quarrel. "Who will be there?"

"Lairds from Cattanach, MacPhail, Shaw, Farquharson, the Ritchies, McCombies and Clan MacThomas."

"And MacPherson."

"Aye."

He frowned. "The day after tomorrow, you say?"

"Aye."

Dominic glanced at Declan. "That doesna leave us much time." Urquhart Castle was a full day's ride.

"We can leave tomorrow."

"The three of us?" Liam asked, although there was no need to ask. Liam and Declan were his lieutenants.

Dominic nodded. "The men can finish up the hunt and head back home." He would have liked to have had a more successful hunt, to fill the smoke room with meat, but it was still summer. There would be more hunts before the harsh winter set in.

"And the woman?"

He glared at his brother. He knew what Declan was asking and it irritated him. Hell, his brother's continued insistence that she was a spy irritated him. "She's coming with us."

Declan snorted, but Liam, at least, knew well enough to stay silent.

"Let's get moving," he said into the silence. "There's much to do if we're to make it to this meeting in time."

* * *

Dominic didn't emerge from his tent for a long while, but when he did, all hell broke loose in the camp. Suddenly the men started rushing about, cleaning the pots and pans and packing them up.

"What's going on?" she asked Ewan, because he was the only one who seemed inclined to speak to her. Still, he didn't meet her eyes.

"We're leaving tomorrow."

"Tomorrow?"

"Aye."

"Are we going back to Castle Dar?" That thought was exciting. She'd only seen pictures of her ancestral home, and even then, it had been ruins. How thrilling would it be to see it in its glory? In person?

"The lads and I are heading back. But the laird is going west. And you're going with him."

She frowned and glanced at where Dominic was overseeing the salting of the venison. He lifted one of the carcasses and tossed it into the cart. His muscles bunched fabulously, snagging her attention. There might have been some drool. She was glad he was taking her with him, wherever they were going. "What's in the west?" she asked.

"Urquhart Castle."

Her heart stopped. Her head whipped around. She stared at Ewan. "What?"

"Urquhart Castle. There's to be a meeting of the lairds."

A meeting of the lairds? Her pulse thrummed. Sweat pricked on her brow.

It would not be a meeting. It would be a massacre.

Even though she knew warning him could ruin everything, certainly destroy any feelings of trust between them, she had to. She had to warn him.

She launched to her feet and ran—*ran*—to Dominic's side. He stilled when she tugged at his sleeve. "I need to talk to you," she said.

He grinned and bent to kiss her. "It will have to wait Maggie-mine. We've got a lot of work to do before we lose the sun."

"Please Dominic. I need to talk to you now."

"About what?"

"This trip to Urquhart. Please. It's urgent."

He studied her expression and his brow rumpled but he nodded to Harry who took up his spot. "What is so urgent?" he asked, brushing off his hands and following her away from the other men. To her annoyance, Declan followed too.

"We need to speak privately."

"Right." He headed for his tent.

Declan paced them. Apparently he did not understand the concept of the word *private*.

She stood in the door of the tent, attempting to block his way, but he just pushed past her.

"What is it, Maggie?" Dominic asked.

She flicked a look at Declan and frowned. "I would prefer to speak to you *alone*."

Declan crossed his arms. "I'm sure you would."

"Darling." Dominic's hands were heavy on her shoulders. "Declan is my lieutenant. Anything you have to say to me, you can say in front of him."

Um, not really. Dominic might believe her—or he might not—but Declan would automatically leap to the dark side. He already suspected the worst of her.

Dominic folded his arms and shot her an encouraging smile. "Well?"

Hell. Declan or not, it needed to be said.

"You cannot go to Urquhart castle."

Dominic blinked. "I...what?"

"You cannot go. It's a trap."

Declan bristled. She ignored him.

"MacPherson is not willing to negotiate with Clan Chattan. He and Cameron are plotting an ambush."

"What?" both brothers barked. It was rather intimidating, the pair of them glowering as they were.

"Why would he do that?" Dominic asked.

"If they take out the leaders of the clans, the confederation will fall apart."

Silence rippled through the room. Dominic's expression went hard. She hated the curl of disdain on his lips. "How do you know this?"

She read it in a book? "I...just know it."

"So you *are* in league with the Camerons?" Declan, singing that same old song.

"If I were in league with your enemies, would I be warning you that they plan to murder you in your sleep?"

"You would if you were trying to trick us into missing the meeting." Declan glared at his brother. "An insult to the MacPherson could also scuttle the confederation."

"MacPherson never intended to join the confederation." This she nearly shouted. "He never forgave Cattanach for not including him in the initial planning. He's been colluding with the lesser clans to form a competing confederation."

Dominic's throat worked. "The...lesser clans?"

"MacGillivray, Davidson, the Macleans of Dochgarroch, Clan Macqueen, the Macintyres of

Badenoch and the Clan Macandrews. The ones not related to Clan Chattan by blood."

Declan stared at her, his nostrils flared, his lips working. "How...do you know this?"

How could she respond? "I just do." The words scraped her throat raw. Because she could tell, not only had she failed to convince them, she'd increased their suspicions about her.

She hated the look on Dominic's face. Hated the coldness in his gaze.

"Leave us Declan," he said. It was a low growl, one not even his brother would defy.

But he did. "Doona listen to her," he said. "Do you need any more evidence of what she is?"

"Leave. Us."

With a huff, Declan spun from the tent. But with his absence, there was no peace.

Dominic's expression was harsh, hard.

"Sit down," he said. His tone was weary, but firm.

She sat. She had to. Her knees were about to fail her. She raked back her hair and sighed. "I know what you're thinking, but it's not true."

"Do you? Do you know what I'm thinking, Maggie?"

Though it was difficult, she met his gaze. "You think I'm in league with your enemies."

"No. That is no' what I am thinking."

She gaped at him. Her lips worked. "Then...what?"

"I'm thinking you haven't been truthful with me. From the start you've lied."

"I have never lied."

"You've not told the whole truth, Maggie."

This she could not deny. "I told you, it's a crazy story."

"I think you need to tell me. You need to tell me everything."

She stared at him, her heart aching, her mind in a whirl. If she told him, he would know, for certain who and what she was. Not a spy or an enemy. But a lunatic.

She wasn't sure which was worse.

"Maggie?"

"I told you the truth when I said I came from a place far to the west, but that's not all."

He sat back. Threaded his fingers. Studied her in steady silence.

"I…" Oh God. "I'm from the future."

His expression did not change. Not by a flicker of an eyelash. That was how she knew he was holding himself in exquisite control.

"Hundreds of years in the future. The book I told you about, *The Macintoshes of Dar*? It's a history book."

Still no reaction. He sat there and stared at her, and she stared right back.

The silence unnerved her.

"I am not crazy."

The pulse at the corner of his left eye ticked.

"I don't know how it happened or why. But I am glad I'm here. I'm so glad I met you. So glad I can save you—"

"Stop. Just stop."

She could not. "If you go, you will die. You and Declan. All your men. Everyone dies there. All but one Macintosh—"

"Maggie. Stop."

"I am not lying." She put out a lip, although she knew pouting was pointless. "I am from the future. How else would I know you're building a new chapel in Dar? Or of the granary fire last spring?

"Those things are hardly secret."

"Would I know you lost your dog in a hunting accident? Or that you commissioned a tapestry in his memory?" He remained stoic and unresponsive. "Dominic, I know many things. I know a great rain will come in the fall. The flood will kill hundreds. The resulting famine will nearly destroy your clan in the winter."

"Are you saying my people will die?"

"If you die, yes. Without your leadership, they are doomed, Dominic. Doomed."

"It is a concerning story indeed. And impossible to prove...until it happens." His lip curled. "Convenient, that."

Ah lord. How could she convince him? Despondent, she opted for babbling historical facts. It was all she had, after all. "Listen to me. I am telling you the truth. Consider this. I know that with the death of Queen Margaret, Scotland has been in turmoil with no one to succeed her. I know next year, with the support of King Edward, John Balliol will become King of Scotland." His nose twitched as though he didn't care for this news. "But he won't be king for long. When he revolts against Edward, a full-fledged rebellion breaks out against England, led by William Wallace."

His brow quirked. "Wallace?"

"Do you know him?"

"We've met. He's a good man."

She sighed. "It doesn't end well for him. But at least they made a movie of his life."

"A movie?"

"Never mind. Point is, I know lots of things, Dominic. Things that have happened and things that are coming. And I'm not evil or crazy or touched. I have to believe God sent me here for a reason. And I have to believe it is to save your life. Please don't go to Urquhart Castle. Please don't walk into an ambush."

"I willna."

She nearly collapsed in relief. "Oh, thank God."

"Now that you've warned us, we shall be on our guard."

Well, fuck.

She reached over, set her hand on his and sighed. "I know it's hard to believe. But it's true."

"I know *you* believe it's true."

She could see it in his eyes. "I'm not mad. I can prove it to you if you give me a chance."

"Prove it?"

"It's August, right?"

He sighed. "Aye."

"What is the date?"

"Maggie—"

"Please, Dominic."

"It is the 22nd of August."

"On the 25th, just three days from now, there will be a partial eclipse of the sun."

"What is that?"

"The moon will move between the earth and the sun. For two minutes, maybe a little more. But you will be able to see it in the sky. Would that convince you?"

"We doona have three days. We need to leave tomorrow."

"But if it happens, if you see it, will you believe me?" *Oh, please. Please.* She didn't know why she needed this so desperately, why she needed him to believe her, but she did.

"All right. If the moon blots out the sun, I will have to agree that you have some knowledge of the future."

Yes! Thank God. All she had to do was keep him alive for three days. And then he would know she was telling the truth. But he was determined to leave in the morning.

She had to make sure he did not.

CHAPTER SEVEN

DOMINIC'S MIND REELED AS HE STOOD AND LEFT HIS TENT. LEFT her. He needed to walk. He needed to think. He could not do so in her presence.

How could he have been so wrong about her?

His heart told him she was the one he'd been waiting for. The woman he'd always dreamed of finding. A perfect connection, a delicious oneness…

But her story was insane.

What was more insane was the fact that a part of him didn't care. Part of him wanted her no matter what—which was frightening indeed. He was the laird of his clan. His people's survival depended upon him, on his decisions, on his good judgement.

How could his desire for her, for any woman eclipse his responsibility to his clan?

Perhaps Declan was right. Perhaps she had bewitched him, stolen his sanity. She had touched him for certain, touched him deeply.

Because even as he was confronted with the undeniable evidence that she was unhinged, he wanted her. Trusted her. He suspected the unfamiliar feeling churning in his heart and soul—the hunger, the need, the blind yearning—might be love.

He hoped that did not indicate a lunacy of his own.

If he were sensible, he would listen to his brother. Send her back with the men to Dar and have them lock her away in the dungeon until he could discover the truth about her.

Indeed, the idea had merit.

Especially since she insisted they were headed for an ambush.

That thought sent a cold bolt through his gut. If they were walking into some violent clash of clans, he did not want her there. He could not guarantee her safety should a melee erupt.

Aye. Perhaps he should send her back to the castle.

Where she would be safe.

With this decision made, his soul ceased its churning, and he turned his mind to other things. Part of her story resonated within him. He'd never trusted MacPherson. Something about his beady eyes, his flickering attention, that half smile that never seemed sincere.

He'd been voluble about his disgruntlement when Dougal Dall, chief of the clan, had not included him in the initial meetings. There were rumors of his efforts to form a competing confederation amongst the clans who had been excluded from the alliance. That part of her story held water. Indeed, it validated the concerns that had been swirling in his mind about MacPherson. And her assertion that the bastard was collaborating with their enemy? That rang true as well.

And such familiarity of the political underpinnings of the clan was not common knowledge. He had no idea how she had come to have this information, but he could not deny that her warnings made sense.

"Dominic." His brother's voice behind him scuttled this thoughts.

He turned with a sigh. "Aye?"

"What are you thinking?"

He scrubbed his face with a palm. "I'm thinking you may have been right about her."

To his credit, Declan did not smirk. "I'm sorry." A simple statement, it should not have wounded him as it did.

"I do believe she's telling the truth about MacPherson, though. I do believe danger awaits us at the meeting."

Declan nodded. "Aye."

"I think it would be wise if we take all the men, except for Ewan and Harry. They can return to the castle with the cart and…"

"And?"

"And Maggie. She canna come with us." Not only was it unsafe, he couldn't take the chance that she might, indeed, be an agent of the enemy. The thought slayed him.

"I think that is wise." His brother clapped him on the shoulder.

"We need to prepare the men." This was no longer a political mission. They were now in battle mode.

"Aye."

And as for Maggie? Tomorrow he would say his farewells to her. But tonight?

Tonight he would indulge in her.

If she was right about the ambush, it might well be their last night together.

* * *

Maggie didn't understand Dominic's expression when he pushed into the tent. He stood there and stared at her as though he could not stare at her enough. The intensity, the harshness in his gaze sent a shiver of excitement through her.

Without a word, he pulled off his jerkin and his tunic. They fell to the ground. His breeks followed. He stood before her — magnificent, beautiful, irresistible — gaze aflame. Though the sight discombobulated her, she rushed to follow suit, unbuttoning her blouse and wriggling out of her bra and jeans.

When she was naked she went up on her knees before him. Her attention was locked on one thing and one thing only.

His cock.

It stood high before him, though with its weight — fully engorged as it was — it leaned a little to the left. It was perfect. Long, hard, ready. A bead of dew glistened at the tip.

She needed to taste him.

She set her hand on his stony thigh and drifted upward. His muscles bunched and he hissed a breath as she made her intentions clear. Though his body was delectable, though his skin was smooth and prickled with manly hair, she did not dally. She scudded her palm up and over his belly, and she enclosed him in her fist.

Damn.

He was like an iron rod, wrapped in velvet.

She pumped him once, slowly, gently. His growl rumbled through the tent. Or it might have been a plea of some kind. Easing up on her knees, she leaned forward and lapped at that tempting tip. He lurched. His fingers threaded through her hair, locked against her scalp.

He spoke not a word, but she knew what he wanted.

She wanted it too.

Sucking in a deep breath, she took him in. Took him deep.

"Christ." A whisper.

Never before had she tasted something so delicious, so enticing, so heart-wrenchingly sweet. He filled her mouth with his manhood, filled her senses with his scent. Filled her soul with his essence.

She played with him, toyed with him. Nibbling and sucking and licking. All the while, she held on to him at the root, working him ruthlessly. She could have nursed him, tormented him all night with this leisurely lust, but he was not patient in the least.

As she clenched his ass for leverage, as she reached around and touched a tender spot, he roared and wrenched away.

"Nae." A growl.

She affected a pout. "But I want to."

"Nae." He came down before her on his knees and cupped her cheeks. Kissed her. "Where did you learn such wicked things Maggie-mine?"

She grinned. "I read it in a book."

His eyes widened. "What kinds of books do they have in Seattle?"

"You'd be surprised."

"No doubt I would."

But this was small talk, a distraction, a conversation that meant nothing and went nowhere. Simply a chance for him to regain his composure, his control as he laid her back on the furs and began a wicked torment of his own.

His mouth was like a forge, heating her, enflaming her everywhere it touched. And it touched her everywhere. *He* touched her everywhere. Her shoulders, her hips, her toes. He spent much time on the tender underside of her knees, which had her writhing before him. This, of course, only incited him to greater mischief.

He turned her over, and explored her back side; to her dismay, he seemed obsessed with the same tender spot she had dandled.

With a laugh, she rolled back and grinned at him. "Nae," she said. And then she opened her legs to him and his attention dropped. Locked. His nostrils flared. He flicked a look at her—one that sent a fire raging in her belly—and then settled between her thighs.

She sucked in a breath as he opened her with this thumbs. He blew a breath on her heated skin and she moaned. But that delight was nothing to the slow and steady lap of his tongue. Ah, heaven. He teased her clit, making agonizing circles around the straining flesh. She fisted her fingers in his hair and yanked when he teased her too long. It was more than she could bear. It was hellish and heavenly and she needed, wanted—

Ah God. Yes.

He closed his lips around her and sucked. Her body seized. It was a small orgasm, but came from deep within. A pre-shock, perhaps, of the temblor to come.

He continued to work her, kiss her, nibble and lap as he slid two fingers into her. They filled her. Filled her deliciously.

"Ah," he murmured around her. "So wet. So ready."

Oh yeah. "Fuck me, Dominic."

She should have kept quiet. His head jerked up. He stared at her. "What did you say?"

"Fuck me. Now."

His nostrils flared. His ferocity surged. Even as she watched, he turned from man to beast. He rose up over her, but he did not sink in as she had hoped. Instead, he flipped her over, gripped her hips and yanked her up against him. "Like this?" he growled. "Do you want me to fook you like this?"

Excitement screamed through her. "Yes." She rubbed against him, against the hard, hot length of his cock, dampening him with her arousal. "Fuck me like this. Do it—"

Oh. He did.

He did.

Easing back, he fisted his cock and set it at her opening. And then he drove deep.

The wolves in the woods probably heard her scream. She did not care.

It was glorious, delirious and maddening. He touched her core, but did not fulfil her. Something deep within ached, cried out for more.

He withdrew and lunged again; she met him halfway, rocking her hips in a frenzy of passion. Again. And again and again. Wilder. Harder. Deeper.

Faster.

Passion rose quickly, taking them both to the top of the cliff, right to the edge. They clung there, together. Both trying to stave off the calamity, but both rocketing inexorably closer to disaster.

The sound of flesh slapping flesh surrounded them, conjoined with the wet percussion of his thrusts, with their moans and sighs and exhortations, one to the other.

"Do it. Harder."

"God, woman. You drive me wild."

"Shut up and fuck me."

"I am."

"Harder. Yes. More. More. More."

And then…and then. Ah. His body bunched. His cock swelled. His groan echoed in her ear. One final thrust, one magnificent in its fury and desperation and breadth. And he hit that spot. Hit it hard and completely and perfectly.

And the orgasm that had been stalking her, pounced. Devoured her. Took her fully.

Glory and bliss rained through her. She devolved into a quivering mass of muscles and bones. She was aware of his groans, the continued surges of his hips as he emptied into her, but the physicality of it seemed far away, removed from her as though she barely clung to her body. As though her soul had ascended. And he was there with her. A manic and glorious comingling, a spiral of colors and sensations and intimacy that far transcended the simple act of joining bodies.

In that moment, in that shard of time, she knew.

She knew.

She loved him with all her heart.

With everything in her.

She loved him and she would do so until the day she died.

Which was a pity really.

Because tomorrow he would hate her.

* * *

She waited until he was asleep before she found her clothing and dressed.

It took every ounce of self-control not to kiss him before she left. But she couldn't wake him. That would spoil her plan, and her plan could not fail. His life depended on it.

Sucking in a breath, she slipped from the tent and skittered through the shadows of the night. But for the snores rising from the tents, and from the lone guard by the fire, it was quiet. She made her way along the tree line to the spot where the horses were tethered. Keeping one eye on the sleeping camp, she untied them one by one, and then led them to the south.

Perhaps it was a foolish plan, stealing their horses. But if God was with her—and she had to believe he was—they would not find where she'd hidden them until it was far too late to make the meeting at Urquhart. Or at the very least, cause them to miss the massacre.

She couldn't contemplate the thought of losing Dominic. Not now that she knew him as a person, as a man. Her heart could not bear it.

It had been bad enough that she'd mourned his death when he'd only been a sketch to her. If he died in the bloody attack of the Camerons, she would simply not want to continue living.

And if her betrayal cost her his esteem, it was a sacrifice she was willing to make. Hell, had to make.

He had to survive.

She needed him to.

Dawn was just breaking as she made her way back to camp. She should not have been surprised to find it in an uproar. Dominic was pacing and Declan was roaring and the men were skittering around in a flurry.

Some of them caught sight of her and a cry rose up.

She was glad she'd circled around, through the woods to the south, to throw them off the scent. Perhaps when they began looking for the horses, as they would, they would head in the wrong direction.

Declan stormed up to her, his fists tight. His expression was furious. She lurched back at his approach, certain he meant to punch her. But he did not. He spit through clenched teeth, "What have you done?"

She pressed her lips together.

This enraged his fury.

He grabbed her shoulders and shook her. "What have you done you Cameron bitch?"

"Declan." Dominic's tone was flinty and cold. "Unhand her."

It was a relief when those hard fingers released her, but her trepidation flared as she glanced at Dominic. His fury was under control, but barely.

"She stole our horses!"

"Technically, I hid them." Probably foolish, but she felt the distinction was relevant.

Dominic stared at her; she hated the hint of disenchantment in his eyes. But she had to ignore it. She had to. It was for the best. "Why did you do that?"

"You know why, Dominic. I couldn't let you go."

"That again?" Declan blew out a snort. He raked his hair. "Bluidy hell, Dominic. I told you we should have tied her to a tree."

"Aye. You did." Oh lord. His tone sent shivers through her belly. He turned to her, indomitable, cold, hard, but his voice was incongruously gentle. "Where are the horses Maggie?"

"I hid them."

"Where?" This, from Declan.

She forced a smile, although one was not called for. "The point of hiding things is not telling where you hid them."

He lunged at her. He nearly reached her, but Dominic held him back. He shot a dark look at each of them, one after the other.

"Send the men to find the horses," he snapped at his brother. She can't have taken them far. "And you?"

She blinked at his vehemence.

"You come with me."

CHAPTER EIGHT

FURY SCOURED HIM.

He doubted he'd ever been so enraged. But then, he'd never felt so betrayed.

Odd that. Living in the highlands, surrounded by clans who stole his cattle and raided his crofts, beset with neighbors who would not think twice about kidnapping a wayward lass or lying straight to a rival's face…he'd never felt so betrayed.

Probably because he'd trusted her. Against his better judgement, he'd trusted an outsider.

He would never make that mistake again.

Without a word he led her to his tent. When she slowed, dragging her feet, he took her arm in a firm grip and hustled her along. He didn't have much time before his wrath worked free, before his rage erupted, and he didn't want his men to see him like that. Didn't want them to see him flay her.

It would only incite them. They were all furious with her as well. No telling what they might do or say if he did not remove her from their presence.

A man's horse was inviolate. It was an unwritten rule they would never be touched or harmed or stolen.

Anyone who dared to break such a convention knew his peril.

Horse thieves were hanged.

The thought of her pretty neck snapping beneath the weight of her crimes horrified him. It did not, however, supplant his anger.

He pushed her into the tent, with perhaps too much force. She skidded backwards and landed on the pallet. She stared up at him with wounded eyes, but he refused to feel a hint of remorse. She'd landed on the soft furs, after all. The furs where, but a few hours earlier, they had tangled

He had to look away. His glance fell on the whiskey.

With harsh movements, he uncorked the bottle and poured himself a stiff draught. It burned on the way down.

"Dominic—"

"Silence!" She dared speak? Did she not know what menace she taunted?

She lurched back as though he'd slapped her; a sliver of guilt skewered him. He brushed it away. Weakness was foolish. He should have known.

"What are you going to do with me?" This she asked in a tiny voice, one that made him shudder.

He stared at his drink, refused to look at her. "That depends on whether or not we find the horses."

"If you don't?"

"You'll hang."

She made a noise, something strangled and wounded. "Hang?"

She would never hang. He wouldn't allow it. But she had to understand the weight of what she'd done. Not only had she delayed a very important journey, she'd committed the most heinous crime of all. "'Tis what we do with horse thieves." He dared a glance at her. "Is this not so in Seattle?"

"We don't have many horses in Seattle."

He wanted to ask how they got around in this mythical place, but he didn't. He did not want to engage in a conversation with her. He did not want to diffuse his ferocity. He could not allow himself to be fooled again.

"We hang horse thieves here."

"I didn't steal them."

"Did you no'?"

"I just *hid* them. You'll find them." Her lashes flickered. "Eventually."

"And did it occur to you that we may no' find them?"

"You will. I'll take you to them tomorrow."

His muscles locked. Irritation at her nonchalance prickled his nape. He glared at her. "Tomorrow?"

She nodded. "Tomorrow."

He whirled and paced, raking his hair with shaking fingers. "And what is the point of all this?"

Her answer was soft, tremulous, but he heard it. "To keep you safe, of course."

He whirled around. "Goddamn it Maggie! I am perfectly safe. My men have been warned. They've been trained. They are prepared to meet any foe."

"If you go there, you die."

"I should turn you over my knee." Oh, he wanted to. So badly. But he'd never struck a woman and he feared his anger would overcome his restraint. In so many ways. He could not allow himself near enough to touch her or disaster might prevail.

That she shot him a minxish grin didn't help.

Damn her. She was too alluring by far.

He pushed out of the tent and bellowed at Ewan, though he was near enough that bellowing was not necessary. "Tie her up," he said. "And make damn sure she doesna get away, or I'll have your guts for garters."

And then he stormed off, in the wake of his men, who were heading to the south to find their damn horses.

On foot.

* * *

It was dusk by the time they found the beasts. It took all day because apparently, Maggie was even more duplicitous than he'd imagined. She hadn't taken them to the south. She'd taken them to the north.

After a long, tiring, frustrating morning, marching through the summer heat, they'd returned to the camp and done what they should have done earlier. Examined the tracks more carefully.

Yes. They did lead off to the south, but then they veered off into a burn and didn't appear again. When they followed the little stream to the north, they eventually found another trail curving toward the west, and into the woods. And there by a small pond, surrounded with a lea of fresh grass, they found their horses, safe and hale.

At least she'd had the heart to make sure they had water and food.

But that was small consolation.

As they mounted up and led the string of horses back to camp, Dominic realized she'd gotten what she wanted. He would not make it to Urquhart in time for the meeting. Damn it all.

They would leave at first light, and ride hard, though. Perhaps they would not be too late to salvage something.

If indeed it was a true meeting of the minds...and not an ambush.

He thrust that thought aside and focused on his annoyance at her ploy.

He was glad he'd decided not to take her with him. He was glad he was sending her back to Dar, to languish in the dungeon until he returned. He hoped it taught her a lesson. He hoped it taught her that no one betrayed Dominic Dundragon without paying the price.

Although what he would do with her when he returned...?

Hell.

He had no idea.

* * *

She heard the horses coming and blew out a breath.

She knew Dominic was angry, but she could also tell, from the falling shadows, that evening was upon them. It was too late for them to leave. They would not be in Urquhart in the morning.

They would miss the massacre.

That was worth any price.

She hoped when he came in, settled down for the night, he would be calmer. He would be willing to listen to her once more.

But he never came back.

Night fell and silence settled over the camp and he never came to her.

He left her there, tied to the pole in his tent. All alone.

It was the longest night of her life.

But morning was worse.

She could hear the men rising, packing up, chattering. She could smell breakfast cooking. But no one came to untie her.

Her wrists were sore, her arms, having been in the same position all night, ached. Her bladder was full.

When Ewan came through the tent flap, she nearly collapsed in relief, but even though she called out to him, he ignored her, merely collecting Dominic's things and carting them outside.

He came in several times, until everything was gone except the pallet and furs on which she rested.

Her belly went hard. Her blood went cold. Were they going to *leave* her here? The thought palled. When the sounds outside rose, calls of farewell, the thunder of hooves, she nearly broke into tears.

She knew he'd left her.

Felt it in the hollow core of her being. A coil of dread rose to take the place of hope.

Yes, he was a grown man. He could take care of himself. But she couldn't help thinking, he needed her. Needed her to keep him safe.

It didn't occur to her that she needed him for the same reason. Not until Ewan and Harry stepped into the tent. Their expressions were blank, but not blank enough that she did not sense their anger, their distrust of her.

"Have they gone?" she asked, though she knew the answer. It hardly mattered that they didn't answer. Her gaze fixated on the knife Ewan held. Trepidation skittered through her.

Oh lord. How angry was Dominic? Or was it not anger? Was it mercy to send his man in to slit her throat? To save her from hanging?

Fear clutched at her. She struggled to catch a breath. Sweat prickled on her brow. She was tied. Helpless. She couldn't even fight—

But Ewan strode past her to the tent pole and cut her tether. It wasn't lost on her that he did not untie her hands. He jerked her to her feet and led her from the tent, while Harry collected the bedding and broke down the structure.

To her shock—once her eyes adjusted to the glare of the sun—the camp was empty. Utterly deserted. Even the fire had been doused. All that remained was the cart filled with salted deer carcasses. Ewan towed her in that direction.

She stopped short and braced herself for his tug when he noticed she was not obediently following him. He frowned at her.

"I need to use the bathroom," she said.

He shot a look at Harry and then changed directions toward the woods. He didn't take her deep in, but paused beside the first bush. When she opened her mouth to protest, his frown darkened. "Hurry up."

She blew out a sigh and tried to move quickly, but it was difficult with her hands tied before her. She knew better than to ask him to release her. His expression made clear he'd been commanded to keep her on a short leash.

Literally.

By the time she was finished, Harry had stowed the tent. Ewan led her to the cart and lifted her into the back. She could hardly complain—the seat in the front was barely big enough for the two burly Scotsmen—but seriously? Did they expect her to travel all the way to Castle Dar on top of dead meat? The smell alone was revolting.

"I think I'm gunna barf."

"Be silent, woman," Harry snapped.

"Seriously. I think I'm going to be sick."

"I told you we should have listened to Declan and gagged her," Harry muttered.

"The laird said to be gentle with her."

"I doona think he meant it. He was glowering at the time."

"He's glowered a lot…since *she* came along." Ewan shot her a dark look over his shoulder. He slapped the reins and the cart lurched forward.

Maggie's stomach lurched too. She groaned. "Can you at least give me something to eat?" Maybe that would settle the bile churning in her belly.

Harry blew out a sigh and pulled an oatcake from his sporran, handing it to her without a word. She took it and nibbled at it and tried to be grateful. Honestly. It could be worse. Couldn't it?

She tried to look on the bright side. She had managed to delay Dominic's departure, possibly saved him from MacPherson's perfidy. She hadn't been hanged. That was always a positive. And it was a lovely day for a cart ride through Scotland. Folks at home would have paid big bucks for something like this. Probably.

"Where are we going?" she asked. She hoped they were following the men to Urquhart, but she doubted it.

Ewan confirmed her suspicions. "We're going back to Castle Dar."

Yes. What she'd expected. But when Harry leaned back and shot her a malicious grin and added, "And you, wee lass, are heading for the dungeon," she was surprised indeed.

All of a sudden, the day was not so very fine after all.

* * *

They rode fast and hard, though Dominic took a care with their horses, making sure to rest and water them regularly. They made good time, but he knew they would miss the meeting. There was no way they could make it. If only there were a ferry across the loch. But there was not, and Loch Ness was large and deep. They had to ride through Glen Mor to the west, then north to Lochend, and then back down to Kilmore on the west bank.

Evening was falling by the time they caught sight of the fluttering banners of the encampment, far in the distance.

When there was such a gathering of clans, the influx was often too great for a castle to accommodate, so they made camp in the surrounding fields. These reunions were infrequent, as they all lived far from each other, so most stayed for days. There were usually games of skill, much drinking and excellent food. A fair-like atmosphere prevailed.

Dominic was gratified to see that everyone had not left; perhaps he could still meet with MacPherson.

If nothing else, he was more than ready to rest his bones, have a warm meal and a stiff drink.

But as they came closer, something felt off. He slowed his mount.

"What is it?" Declan asked.

Dominic glanced at the sky, to the wheeling birds. He scanned the camp for movement. There was none.

"Do you see anyone?"

Declan frowned. "Nae."

No men. No women. No songs or laughter wafted to them on the wind, as they should. Only the caws of those birds.

He glanced at his men, and as one, they drew their swords. They rode closer to the camp, splitting into two to circle at a distance. Ten large tents. No fires. No horses. Nothing.

Dominic shot a glance at the castle, about a league away on the banks of the river. The castle itself was held by John Comyn, Lord of Badenoch, a contender for the Scottish crown, but Comyn was rarely in residence here. The castle, too, seemed eerily deserted.

He lifted a leg and slipped from his saddle. "Shall we investigate?"

His men nodded and followed suit. But not one of them spoke.

They crept into the camp, moving slowly and silently, checking each tent as they passed. Oddly enough, they were all deserted. The first sign they had that something was awry, was a boot.

Declan's brow darkened as he bent to pick it up. He issued an eep and tossed it away, rearing back in revulsion.

"What is it?" Dominic asked.

His brother, who was normally as staunch as they came, vomited into the grass. "The leg…" A gasp. "Was still in it."

Holy hell.

Dominic gestured to his men and they fanned out, looking for any more clues as to what had happened here. His gut tightened.

Had Maggie been right about the ambush? Had she been right all along?

"Here!" Liam cried from the large tent in the center of the assemblage. The others rushed to his side. "Here. They're in here."

Slowly Dominic pulled back the tent flap. And he gagged himself. Not only because the first soulless eyes he saw were those of his friend Brody Ritchie. Not only because the tent was littered with bodies—and body parts—and bathed in blood. But because with the heat of the summer sun baking the corpses, the stench was horrific. It was surprising he hadn't smelled this coming in.

They covered their mouths and made their way around the perimeter of the tent and the extent of this atrocity became clear. The men had been gathered here. Drinking, perhaps. Laughing. Tossing dice. Their swords were all sheathed. They'd had no clue this was coming. No clue at all.

They had, indeed, been massacred.

"Who do you see?" he called out, but he knew, in his heart, he knew.

"Laird of MacThomas here," Declan called.

"McCombies. And aye, Shaw by his side."

They found Cattanach, with his eyes gouged out and MacPhail and Farquharson as well.

"Any MacPhersons?"

Declan stood. Huffed a sigh. "Nae. No' a one."

Bluidy hell. Bluidy fooking hell!

Fury raged within him, but it battled with an undeniable sense of relief. Whatever or whoever she was, Maggie had been telling the truth. She had known the truth. Or seen it. She wasn't mad. Or a traitor.

But there was no time to reflect on that now. "We need to go," he clipped. He needed to get home to Dar. No doubt who ever had done this — MacPherson, with Cameron at his back — had noticed he wasn't here. If their intent was a complete annihilation of the Clan Chattan leadership, they would be assembling an army to attack him where he lived.

He turned to Angus. "I need you to ride to Cattanach. Let them know we were late to the meeting, and what we found. What we suspect our enemies are up to. Have them notify all the clans of this treachery. We will all need to rally together to defeat these bastards."

"Aye, laird."

Liam stepped forward. "Let me go with him."

Dominic clapped him on the shoulder. "Nae, cousin. I canna spare you. When we get home, we will need your expertise."

Liam's eyes widened. "Why?"

"Because," he said. "They will be coming for us. They will hit hard and fast."

And Maggie was there. Right in the middle of the danger.

And there was no way to warn her.

Worst of all? He'd sent her there.

CHAPTER NINE

THE SIGHT OF CASTLE DAR RISING ON THE RIDGE OVERLOOKING Loch Dundragon stole Maggie's breath. It was large and magnificent, hewn of stones that glittered silver in the sunlight. The ramparts were high and crenelated; two turrets rose on either side. Banners, bearing the iconic family crest, a fierce dragon, flapped in the wind.

As they'd followed the track in, past the crofts heavy with summer wheat, signs of prosperity were everywhere. Fat villeins, numerous chickens and healthy shaggy cows. The crofters all raised a hand to them and called greetings.

They'd turned the corner on the top of the hill and the plains of Dar spread out before her. The little village, nestled at the base of the hill and there above it, the castle, framed by blue skies and puffy clouds.

It could be a postcard, had they been invented yet.

Maggie gusted a sigh. It was beautiful. It felt like *home*.

As they passed through the village, everyone waved. Tall, braw lads and lasses dressed in the kirtles of the day. They were her people, far-removed, of course. But they were her people.

They crossed the moat and rumbled over the bridge, beneath the gaping portcullis. Maggie tipped back her head and soaked in every detail. The well-oiled chains and the pulleys. The murder holes built into the passage. All exactly as she'd expected it to look. It was fascinating.

The bailey of the castle fascinated her as well. They passed the guard house, the dove cote and the smithy. She could see the gardens and what looked like an apiary on the far side, and the stables to her left. Men and women of all ages bustled about their work. She took it all in with delight.

But apparently, she was not to be allowed delight.

The cart stopped and Ewan hopped out. "Come along, you," he growled, grabbing her ankles and dragging her from the cart by her feet. As unseemly as this treatment was—and his continued use of her tether—Maggie tried to hide her outrage. She'd come to terms with the fact that these men didn't trust her. It was the consequence of her situation and hardly their fault. They were simply trying to protect their people.

Ewan took her arm and led her toward the north tower, but before they reached the steps, a horn blew. The activity in the bailey shot from busy to frenetic, like a beehive, nudged too hard.

"What is it?" she asked, but everyone ignored her. Really ignored her. Ewan and Harry ran back to the portcullis, leaving her standing in the yard. They gestured madly at the villagers who were now streaming into the castle.

One old woman bustled past her, with a basket of vegetables. Maggie grabbed her arm. "What is it?" she asked. "What's happening?"

"'Tis the Camerons," she said. "They are approaching from the east. "It looks as though they've brought an army."

And that quickly, her delight at finally seeing her ancestral home deflated.

They were under attack.

As the last of the villagers scuttled into the keep, the portcullis rolled down in an ominous clank and the men pulled up the bridge over the moat. Men and women — farmers and milk maids, scuttled to the armory and began carting arrows and spears up to the ramparts.

It seemed well-ordered and practiced. Dominic had, perhaps prepared his people for such an event. Or it had happened before.

Pushing through the crowd making their way into the castle proper, Maggie headed for the rampart steps; she took them two at a time.

The men stationed on the wall shot her odd glances, but said nothing as she made her way to Ewan's side. She watched in silence as a wave of armed and mounted men in blue plaids swept across the plain.

It was a breathtaking sight, but not in a good way. They pounded closer and then halted, about three hundred feet from the castle wall.

"What do they want?" she asked in a whisper.

Ewan frowned down at her. "You shouldna be here."

"Why not?"

She expected him to spew some nonsense about women being helpless and frail, but he just said, "The Macintosh would no' like it. He wanted me to keep you safe."

"I'm perfectly safe."

His nostrils flared. "This is an attack, in case you haven't noticed."

"I have noticed. I've also noticed they stopped out of range." While the Macintosh arrows could not reach them, the enemy, in turn, could not hit the broad side of the castle...at least, not from that distance. "Besides, I'll have you know, I wrote an entire chapter in my Masters thesis on siege warfare tactics of the Middle Ages."

"The middle what?" His brow rumpled. "I have no idea what that means."

"It means I can help. So quit bugging me and let me think." She thrust her hands out. "And untie me."

He frowned at her, but he complied. Then he turned to his men and began barking orders for them to finalize their defense. Maggie studied the movements of their enemies, as they surrounded the castle in a semi-circle and started setting up camp. Several large carts followed them at a distance. One carried the familiar lines of a trebuchet and another, with a domed wooden roof, was undoubtedly their battering ram machine.

It was the beast that followed that made her heart lodge in her throat. These Camerons were serious. An enormous siege tower rolled onto the plain. It moved slowly on lumbering wheels, but that didn't make it less ominous. She knew the damage a siege tower could wreak on a castle.

As menacing as the battering ram and the trebuchet could be, the tower was the real threat. They had to incapacitate it at once.

She turned to Ewan. "Do you have a ballista?" Like an overgrown crossbow, a ballista had tremendous force and could catapult lethal bolts much farther than a bow and arrow. It was usually used in offense, sapping walls and taking out castle defenses. But a weapon was a weapon. She would use everything they had to fight off this incursion.

"Aye."

"Excellent. And a marksman with very good aim?" At Ewan's nod, she pointed at the siege tower. "Have him target the wheels." They were large, to carry the weight of the wooden tower.

"The wheels, my lady?"

She ignored the fact that he'd accidentally granted her a title of respect. There was hardly time to gloat about winning him over. "Yes. If we can send several bolts straight on into those wheels, they won't be able to move it. The tower will be useless to them." As useless as a booted car in impound. "And get some more oil up here. We'll need it when they drop their ladders." They would likely be dampened, or covered with wet hides, but oil burned through hides. Men burned too. If they tried to breach the walls, she had no compunction about giving them a hot oil treatment.

She scanned the woods in the falling evening, mentally calculating distances between targets and cover. "Ewan, do you have escape tunnels?" Most castles did. Escape tunnels, sapping tunnels and secret sally ports.

He gaped at her. "Do you want to escape?"

She snorted a laugh. "No. But we can send our best archers out once it gets dark. They can hide in the woods around the enemy encampment and then, upon our signal, send flaming arrows into their camp."

"Flaming arrows?"

"Tell them not to aim for the men," she said. They were far too easy to miss. "Aim for their tents and supply stores." Demoralizing the enemy was rule number one in warfare, according to Richardson. She was so glad she'd read his book. "And target their trebuchet and their battering ram as well." All those weapons were made of wood. It was probably folly to imagine a few arrows could destroy them, but it didn't hurt to try. A pity it was too dangerous to send a man into their midst to douse the weapons with oil first.

But then an idea blossomed. She snapped her fingers and grinned at Ewan.

"What?" He stared at her, thoroughly bemused.

"A Molotov cocktail."

"A what?"

"We send the archers in with jars filled with oil, which they launch into the weapons store, and onto those machines. Then follow with flaming arrows."

Ewan's nostrils flared. "You are a fierce lass."

"Oh, and I want oil poured on the moat as well."

"On the moat?"

"If we need to, we can light it. No doubt they'll try to breach the walls with ladders."

Ewan shook his head. "Where did you learn all this?"

She merely smiled sweetly in response. "Oh, and one more thing. Was that an apiary I noticed by the garden?"

He blinked. "Aye."

"I would like to speak to your beekeeper."

His brows knit, but he nodded.

She clapped her hands. "Well? Come on. Let's get moving."

She had a castle to save.

* * *

Bluidy hell.

They were too late.

The Camerons were already here.

Dominic peered over the rise at a sight that curdled his blood. The enemy had his castle surrounded. Their bluidy blue banners snapped merrily in the wind. Thank God it was nearly nightfall and they weren't quite set up for an attack. Torquil would most likely wait until dawn. For now, he had his drummers playing and his men chanting and pounding their spears in an attempt to frighten the castle denizens.

He'd trained his people, warned them what tactics an enemy might take. He hoped they remembered his exhortations. He also hoped that Angus was fleet of foot. That he would bring reinforcements from the other clans. Judging from the army Cameron had amassed, they would need help fighting them off.

For now, he had to get into the castle.

It was a damn shame he had his best strategists with him. Between Declan and Liam, no one was better.

"Come on," he whispered. Voices carried on the night air. "To the sally port." It would take them a while, as he knew they had to go on foot, and circle the valley. If they were lucky, they'd get there by dawn.

As they made their way through the woods, parallel to the enemy's camp, campfires flared and the Camerons settled in for the night. Dominic knew it was far too soon to feel relief, but he was glad they had not elected to attack at once.

No doubt, they felt confident that their presence would be intimidating enough to keep their prey on edge all night.

To his surprise, he saw an arrow, one lone flaming arrow arch from the ramparts and through the sky. It landed woefully short of the enemy camp, thudding impotently into the dirt. His chest clenched. Who the hell was running things on the ramparts? Did they not know the range of an arrow?

But then, to his surprise, other arrows began to fly — and not from the castle. From the woods. A fiery rainstorm of them. And they kept coming. He watched in shock as the blazing arrows landed on the Cameron tents throughout the camp, on their supply carts and their war machines, wreaking havoc.

One arrow hit their trebuchet and it exploded into flames.

Cries rose and men scattered, batting at flames and running for water.

Dominic bit back a smile.

Brilliant.

Brilliant strategy.

Who was running the defenses from the ramparts?

Whoever it was, they would be joining his elite team of warriors…if they all survived this.

With the Camerons distracted, Dominic and his men raced through the woods toward the sally port, the secret gate that led into the castle. Dawn was just breaking as Dominic pulled a stone from the wall and pulled out the hidden key. He fit it in the lock. It creaked as he turned it.

The door had not been used for decades and the gate had rusted. There was a mound of dirt blocking its path. Dominic set his weight against the bars and pushed it open. It took a while to create a passable gap.

He eased through and his men followed.

Liam was the last through. He set his shoulder to the grate to push it closed. It resisted. "I'll lock it," he said. "You go on."

Dominic nodded and sped up the stairs, through the second and third gates, which opened and locked using a series of hidden levers.

They emerged in the larder, behind a shelf of crockery and raced through the castle halls into the bailey. Then they bounded up the rampart steps.

Dominic stopped short.

Maggie—glorious and fierce, with her hair streaming out behind her—stood by Ewan, barking out commands.

And his men were obeying her.

It took a moment for this to sink in.

He cleared his throat.

She whipped around. Her eyes widened and her lips parted. Damn, she was beautiful in the soft morning light. A flush rose on her cheeks. "Dominic."

"Maggie. I...what are you doing?"

Apparently she did not care for his tone. She set her fists on her hips and snapped, "Mounting the defense of your castle."

He glanced at the small trebuchet, one they kept for defense and target practice, and then at three small bundles wrapped in rags. Oddly enough, they...hummed. "Ah... What...what are these?"

She grinned. It was a heinous, evil, wicked grin. "A wake-up call." She turned to Ewan. "Are we ready to launch?"

Ewan glanced at him for guidance—Dominic shrugged—and Ewan nodded. "Let's do it."

The trebuchet released its first strange missile. As it flew through the air, the rag wrapping it whipped away. The missile fell dead center in the enemy camp. But before it landed, Maggie was already repositioning the catapult and placing the second missile gently in the cup.

A yowl rose from the camp below. Dominic glanced that way and his eyes widened. Camerons scattered, hither and yon, howling and batting the air around them.

"Fire two," Maggie warbled. Her tone held far too much glee.

She quickly re-sighted and fired the third and final missile. In short succession, those missiles landed on either side of the camp with similar results.

"What, may I ask, did you send them?" He had to ask. Whatever it was, it was ingenious and evil. The Camerons were in chaos.

"Just a little something sweet." Like her smile. He longed to kiss her but this was hardly the place.

"What?"

"Beehives," Ewan said.

Dominic looked out at the field again and his lips quirked. A chuckle rose up within him, and then a laugh. It rang across the ramparts and over the bee-infested lea.

Below, Torquil Cameron glared up at him. And then he shook his fist.

And then, of course, he howled and swatted at his neck. But it was far too late. The bees had found him.

CHAPTER TEN

Battle was invigorating. Maggie found it suited her well. And not just because she'd spent a lot of time studying the history of military strategy, but because it was a damn lot of fun anticipating an enemy's move and squelching it before it could come to fruition.

She had been right about the clumsy tower. Two iron bolts fired straight into the treads of the front wheels stopped it short. That it stalled close enough for them to rain fire upon it was an added bonus.

They launched the Molotov cocktails first of course, soaking the structure in oil. When the flaming arrows hit it, the conflagration was spectacular. They had the same luck with the cart carrying the battering ram.

The poor Camerons were being trounced. When a ladder came up over the castle walls, her men doused it in more oil and lit it on fire. Then they pushed it back down with long spears. Whenever the enemy amassed to launch another attack, they received another bumble of bees. Any time they ventured too close, her archers let fly.

Just before midday, the enemy drew back, but Maggie didn't have any delusions that they were giving up. Indeed, the silence was unnerving.

"What do you think they're up to?" she asked.

Dominic, who had remained by her side, set his arm around her shoulders. "They probably need a rest. So do you."

She frowned at him. "This is warfare. There's no naptime in warfare."

"It concerns me that you are enjoying this so much." But he said this with a smile.

"It's kind of fun."

"Will you at least come down into the bailey and eat?" A table with food and drink had been set up for the fighting men along one wall.

"All right. But I want to know the moment anything changes."

Dominic glanced at Declan who stepped up to take his position. "You heard the lady. The moment anything changes."

"Aye." Declan fixed his gaze on her. She was gratified to see it lacked his usual derision. In fact, there might have been a hint of admiration in his eyes.

Dominic led her down the stairs, holding her hand to keep her steady. Though she hardly needed his help, she liked the feel of his fingers laced in hers. "You were right, you know."

"Hmm?"

"About the ambush."

She nodded. "I know."

His head whipped around and he gaped at her. But then he chuckled. "Are you right all the time?"

"No."

"Thank God for small mercies."

"I didn't know the Camerons would attack." Indeed, they hadn't. At least, not in the history *she* knew. But then, she'd changed history, hadn't she? When she'd saved Dominic and his men from the ambush, she'd changed the course of the river. Of course that would cause ripples. It stood to reason the Camerons would attack if they'd failed in their attempt to take out the Macintosh.

She had to wonder what other effects her small act of mercy would have over the next few millennia. Hopefully nothing too drastic. She'd hate to go home and discover something terrible...like the Nazis had won WWII or that Starbucks only served decaf.

The thought palled.

And then another thought hit her and hit her hard.

Go home?

Her stomach clenched at the thought.

Oh, she loved coffee and cheesecake and couldn't say enough about the miracles of fast food restaurants and reality TV, but the prospect of living the rest of her life without Dominic...well, it made her want to weep.

She glanced up at him, studying him. Trying to picture him in Seattle.

An old woman came up to him and handed him a cup. He took it with a smile of thanks and exchanged a word with her, and with another. It was there on his face, his dedication to these people. To his lands.

He would not be happy in Seattle.

He would not be happy leaving his homeland.

He would hate the frustrations of modern times. Traffic and pollution and man's inhumanity to man. Mostly the fact that he would be able to control none of it.

He was very much the kind of man who liked having control of his own destiny. Very few people did in her world, though they liked to pretend they did.

No. If they were to be together, she would have to stay — if he wanted her to stay.

He turned and caught her gaze on him. His smile faded and he came to her, cupped her cheek in his broad palm. "What is it Maggie-mine?"

Ah. She'd never thought to hear those words from him again.

"Have you forgiven me for what I did?" she asked, staring up at him, half afraid he would step away.

He stared at her. "For what? Saving my life? My brother's life?"

"Technically, I just warned you."

"Technically, you saved my life. Without that warning, without your interference, I would no doubt have been slaughtered with my kinsmen."

"You would have been."

"I appreciate what you did. I apologize for my anger at you. Can you forgive me?"

She wrinkled her nose. "That depends."

He paled. His hand shook, just a tad. "On what?"

"Will you believe me next time?"

"I will…but Maggie?"

"Yes, Dominic?"

"Have a care who you share information like this with."

"I…of course."

"Because at best, they'll think you're mad. At worse, they'll accuse you of being in league with the devil."

"You won't let them burn me at the stake, will you?"

Her joke went awry. His expression hardened. "Promise me you will be careful. Promise me you will keep this a secret. I couldna bear it if you were harmed."

Her heart lifted with this declaration. Hardly a loverly vow, but close. "Oh?" She wrapped her arms around his waist and gazed up at him. "Do you like me then? Maybe a little?" It was wrong to tease him, but she couldn't resist.

"You know I like you. A lot."

"I like you a lot too." A whisper, but she barely needed to speak up, as his head was descending. His lips touched hers and it was heaven. There was no telling how much time they might have together, but she wanted to spend every moment she could just here, with him. Like this.

A cry arose to her left and Dominic's head jerked up. His expression twisted in fury.

Maggie glanced in the direction of his glare and was horrified to see a horde of blue-clad Camerons pouring from the castle into the bailey, bristling with weapons.

To her dismay, she saw that one of the men held Liam prisoner with a blade to his neck. Her heart froze.

Oh God.

She had changed the course of the river.

Liam had been the only Macintosh to survive the massacre at Urquhart. He had gone on to be the Laird of Dundragon in Dominic's stead; he had fathered a wealth of sons—one of whom had been her great-great-great-whatever grandfather.

Should Liam die, she would never be born.

She had to do something. Something to save him. She wiped the sweat from her brow as her mind whirled. The sun was cresting the clear sky. The day was hot.

"Macintosh!" One of the Camerons yelled. She took from this that he was the leader. "Stand down or your cousin dies."

At her side, Dominic bellowed, "Torquil, you will hang for this."

"Will I?" Torquil Cameron stepped forward. His face was a moonscape of bumps and bulges that could have been beestings...or an early manifestation of the plague. His features were harsh and lopsided. His eyes were piggish, his nose flat and squat with prominent nostrils. His chuckle was coarse, like gravel. "Word is, ye and yer men killed every laird who attended the convocation. I'll be lauded a hero for taking you down."

"We dinna kill anyone and you know it."

"Yet you are the only laird of the confederation to survive. Convenient, that. A logical pick for chief. Nae doubt the other clans will see it that way."

"Will they?" Dominic pulled himself to full height. "We've sent word to Cattanach telling of your collusion with MacPherson. By now everyone knows of your perfidy."

Torquil's nostrils flared, which was something, because they were already quite large. "You bastard." He lifted his sword and lunged forward.

Trepidation curled in Maggie's chest. Dominic had no weapon and no protection.

Thinking quickly, she lifted a heavy pewter platter from the table and slapped it against his chest just as Torquil's blade landed. It hit hard, sending Dominic back a step, but with all the force Torquil had invested in the blow, the heavy claymore bounced off and clipped him on the ear.

He howled and whirled on her. "Who is this woman?"

"She is mine." A snarl.

Cameron narrowed his gaze on her and lifted his sword.

Maggie knew she had to do something, say something drastic. If she did not, Torquil would attack again and Dominic might die—a platter was not much of a weapon, even though it was made from a toxic metal.

She stepped forward and loudly proclaimed, "Torquil Cameron, if you value your life you will cease and desist at once."

The Cameron froze, mid-swing. He looked her up and down; though his eyes glimmered, his face twisted in a sneer. "I like your bravery lass," he hissed.

"Tis not bravery."

"It is. To challenge me like that."

She laughed, though it cost her. "It's no act of bravery to challenge a dead man."

Silence fell over the bailey with a dull clang.

Cameron peered at her with one eye half closed. "What did you say?" Her hackles rose at his tone, but she could not allow herself to sink into fear. There was far too much at stake.

With all the nonchalance she could muster, she picked up a flagon from the table and took a sip. She couldn't hide her grimace. She didn't care for mead, she decided. It tasted a little bit like honey-flavored shit.

"Woman. Answer me."

She set the cup down. "I think you heard me."

He stilled. His face went a trifle red. He lunged for her.

He should not have. For one thing, he gave her far too much warning. As he approached, she stepped forward, into his attack, grabbed his arm and whipped around, pulling him toward her. Then she used the leverage of his momentum to toss him over her shoulder. He landed on the stone cobbles with a shuddering thud.

As a huge gasp rose up among the gathering, she plucked an errant thread from her sleeve.

"Please doona do that again," she said in a warning tone. She hoped he would be warned, but he was a bull of a man and they tended to be dense. She decided to go on the offense. "I would hate to be the one to end you."

Cameron struggled to his feet and gaped at her.

She met his ominous glower with a simper. "I do deplore violence."

He seemed as though he was considering another rush at her, so she tipped her head to the side and fixed him with an imperious look. "Dinna the Macintosh tell you what I am?"

He glanced at Dominic, whose expression went bleak. "Nae, Maggie-mine. Donna tell him."

"Tell me what?"

"I am no' just a mere lass."

"Are ye no'?"

"I come from a land, far to the west. Beyond the great sea."

The Cameron snorted. "There is no land to the west beyond the great sea."

Maggie sighed and glanced at the sky. She tried to appear blasé in her perusal, but she was not. She had to time this just right...and she sincerely doubted she could, for she didn't know everything. She didn't know everything at all. She had to pray her memory was clear, that some future astronomer hadn't gotten a date or a declination wrong. Her pulse pounded.

"Ah, but there is. A great land. Blessed by God. Flowing with milk and honey. Amber waves of grain and all that."

Torquil narrowed his eyes. It made him look even more like a pig.

"I come from The Emerald City."

Dominic frowned. "I thought you said you came from a place called Seattle?"

"With flying fish," Declan added.

"Aye. But it is also called the Emerald City."

"What sept are you from?"

Um, sept? She cleared her throat. "I belong to a sept called...academia. We spend all our days studying the acts of men."

The Cameron's nose curled. "This tale is entertaining, but does not explain your impudence."

She laughed. "All women are impudent where I come from. And with good reason. We are highly educated." She leaned in and grinned. "And we *know* things."

Many of the men reared back, apparently appalled at the prospect of educated women.

"Why did you call me a dead man?"

"Because. I have foreseen it." She had. Torquil Cameron would be murdered by his brother at the age of thirty-six. Poison, if memory served.

Murmurs rose amongst the Camerons. One or two crossed themselves. Dominic groaned but Maggie flashed him a confident smile.

"You are a seer?"

From the crowd, whispers of "witch" and "succubus" rose. She waggled her fingers at them. "Oh, pish. I am no' a servant of the devil. But I know the good Lord doesna smile upon your betrayal of Clan Chattan."

Torquil bristled. It was not attractive. "I dinna betray Clan Chattan!"

"Did you no'?" She fixed him with what she hoped was an unnerving stare and murmured, "God knows all things, Torquil. He sees all. He can glimpse inside the hearts of men. And his vengeance canna be escaped."

His throat worked. His little piggy eyes shot around.

"Oh, doona worry. It is not my place to punish you for what you have done."

He seemed to gust a sigh of relief.

"But God willna forget."

"You doona speak for God, witch. Tis blasphemy to suggest it."

"Aye. I doona. God speaks for himself. To show his disapproval of your ways, he will send a sign."

Cameron stilled. Stared at her. "A sign?"

"He will blot out the sun." Dear God, she hoped she had her dates right. She hoped she had the time right. From what she recalled the eclipse that had sent the highlands into a frenzy of fear and ominous predictions had occurred about 12:47 GMT on the 25th of August.

It seemed about that time. As far as she could tell. But it hardly mattered. She could not hesitate now, not that she'd begun on this path.

With melodramatic flair, she threw out her arms to the sun.

All the men in the bailey stared at her—including Dominic—but then, slowly, they lifted their gazes to the sky. Silence thrummed for a long long while.

The sun beamed merrily down.

Maggie's heart skittered in her chest. Her throat closed. Sweat beaded on her brow. Still she held her pose.

She hoped her ploy would not be the death of them all.

"Well, fook," Cameron growled after several minutes. "Why are we even listening to this folderol? Kill them all." He pulled out his blade and headed for Dominic.

"No!" Maggie raced between them, shielding her man with her body.

Dominic muttered something foul and thrust her behind him.

Cameron chuckled. "I'll happily gut you too lass, if you've a liking for it. But later, after I've had you and handed you to my men."

She leaned around Dominic's bulk and glared at him. "You are a revolting creature. I'm glad your brother murders you."

From her left, a man squawked. Cameron's eyes lowered. His head swung around and he pinned the red-faced Scotsman with a glower. "It isna true, Torquil!" he wailed. "I would never do such a thing."

"A little advice?" Maggie smirked. "Get a food taster."

It probably wasn't wise to taunt a bear. Especially when he had a sword. A long, sharp sword. His hammy fingers closed around the hilt and he growled, "Shut your lying mouth, bitch."

"How rude," she murmured, mostly to herself, but no one would have heard anyway because just then a hue and cry rose in the bailey.

Also, the sunlight dimmed.

Maggie whirled around to stare at the sky. Her heart lifted as the shadow of the moon rose, blotting out the sun.

Oh, thank God.

Thank God she hadn't screwed up her dates.

* * *

Dominic stared at the sky as the moon swallowed the sun.

He should not have been worried.

He should not be surprised.

He should have known she was right.

She usually was.

He glanced around the courtyard, at all the men, Camerons and Macintoshes alike, who stared in awe at the sky. They were utterly stupefied, Torquil among them.

It would be folly to waste this opportunity. He pulled his dirk from his boot and whipped behind Torquil, setting his knife to his enemy's neck.

"Drop your weapons, all of you."

The Camerons whirled, but taking a cue from their laird, all the Macintosh men sprang into action, surrounding them. A clatter of metal rose as they dropped their dirks and swords.

His pressed the knife into Torquil's neck. "How did you breach the castle?" he asked softly, but in the silence, his question wafted on the air.

"I...ah...through the sally port."

"And how did you know where it was?"

To Dominic's disgust, Torquil's gaze flickered over to his men and landed on Liam. Who paled.

Hell and damnation.

"Liam? It was you?" Liam, who had brought him the news of the deadly meeting? Liam, who had stayed behind to lock the gate? Liam, who stood to inherit everything if Dominic and Declan died?

Fury scoured him.

The look Declan shot him made clear he'd worked it all out too. He hustled over and grabbed his cousin by the arm. Ewan and Harry joined him, making sure Liam could not slither away. Not until justice was dealt out.

"Tie the Camerons up and throw them in the dungeon," he commanded and his men scurried to do his bidding. "I hope your family is inclined to pay a healthy ransom," Dominic muttered to Torquil as they led him away.

He turned to Liam and his nose curled. "As for you..."

"What are you going to do to him?"

Dominic stilled and glanced down at Maggie. The tone of her voice, her panic, the despair, made his blood go cold. He hated the fear in her eyes...because it was on Liam's behalf.

"Why do you care?"

She tugged his sleeve. "Please don't kill him."

Hell. This was more than a soft-hearted woman's worry over someone being hurt. This was more. He didn't like it in the least. "Why not?"

She went up on her tiptoes and whispered in his ear, "Because Dominic. He's my ancestor. If he dies...I will never be born."

He froze.

Oh. God.

Oh God, oh god oh god.

He couldn't bear such a thought.

"Doona worry. I willna kill him. But the punishment must fit the crime."

"I understand."

He turned to Liam, surrounded by a circle of his once-friends, a criminal, an outcast. "Liam MacBain Macintosh. For your crimes of betrayal, I sentence you to—"

"Nae!" Liam issued an inhuman snarl. He lurched forward, breaking the hold the men had on him and, grabbing a fallen dirk, he ran toward Dominic. There was a crazed light in his eye. One that made clear his intention to commit murder.

His intention to murder Dominic.

* * *

It all moved in slow motion. Liam racing toward Dominic. Dominic raising his blade. The two men colliding chest to chest, falling to the ground, rolling. The shouts of the others, a flurry of action, of panic.

Dominic's men converged on the tussle and peeled the two men apart. They were both covered in blood and breathless.

To her horror, Liam collapsed to the ground, with his eyes wide, staring, unseeing at the sky.

And Dominic?

Dominic had a blade buried in his chest. He lay there, still and silent. Limp.

Maggie stared at the horrific scene, unable to speak or move or breathe.

Her mind spun. Her pulse slowed. She felt her field of vision shrinking, shrinking, closing in. Her muscles began to crumple. Her soul shriveled. She could feel herself lightening, as though she might waft away into nothingness.

No. No. No!

She fought to retain consciousness, presence in this world. She would not allow this to happen. She could not.

But she couldn't stop it. Couldn't stop the wheeling of the earth or the racing of her broken heart.

Darkness descended and took her.

She did not know whether to be grateful or to grieve.

CHAPTER ELEVEN

SHE AWOKE IN A DARK ROOM. IT TOOK A MOMENT FOR HER TO get her bearings. For one thing, she was not altogether sure she was alive. If Liam was dead, no doubt she'd faded into some limbo. Wherever it was lost souls went.

But limbo probably didn't have fur coverlets on the beds.

Limbo probably didn't have beds.

She felt around and found a bedside table with a candle and a flint, but she had no idea how to strike a flint, so she fumbled around some more until she found a window and yanked back the heavy drapes.

The moonlight flooded in and she surveyed her surroundings. She was in a modest chamber about midway up the south tower—as far as she could tell. And she was wearing a flowing nightdress.

She tried the door and, delighted to find it not locked, she looked out into the hallway. It wasn't a hallway as much as a curving staircase. Voices wafted down from above, so she headed that way. The staircase ended at a broad door which was open. She peered in and knew this would be the laird's solar. It was a large round room that took up the whole floor of the tower.

Dominic laid on the four-postered bed by the hearth. He was surrounded by several men.

Declan glanced up as she slipped into the room. He blanched. "Ye shouldna be here."

She ignored him. "Is he all right?"

The other men took in her attire and their nostrils flared. Without a word, Declan found a blanket and wrapped it around her shoulders.

"It's just a nightdress, she muttered.

"'Tis not seemly."

She blew out a breath. It was a fricking night dress. It covered her from neck to toes. But still, her attire was the least of her worries. "Is he all right?"

"He hasna woken up."

His chest was broad and bare. The knife had been removed but the wound was open and covered with... Her stomach roiled. "Are those leaches?"

"They are necessary." An old man with a prissy expression sniffed. "To remove the evil humors."

"Take them off."

"I beg your pardon?"

"Take them the fuck off."

The doctor glanced at Declan, possibly in outrage, but Declan nodded. "Do as she says." It gratified her that he took her side.

"Bleeding patients is crucial," the doctor muttered, but he began peeling the nasty leeches off.

Thank God.

Seriously. Who knew where they'd been?

"Bleeding patients only weakens them. What he needs is that wound sewn up. A little antiseptic would not go awry."

The doctor reared back. "I willna be responsible for his health if you doona listen to me."

"Fine," Declan said, leading him to the door.

Maggie was more than happy to see the doctor leave. Though she was far from a medical expert, no doubt she had a better grasp on healthcare than a man who believed in body humors and trepanning. Besides, she'd seen tons of medical dramas on TV.

Through the night, she did everything she could think of—everything she'd learned from Dr. Blake Braxton—from hot compresses to salt washes, but Dominic didn't get better. He didn't awake. By morning, his fever had spiked.

The next day it was worse, and by the third day, it was clear an infection was setting in. The wound was horrendous. Black around the edges and raw inside. What scared her to death was the red stripes fanning out, a sign that the contamination had entered his bloodstream, perhaps leading to sepsis. Sepsis was fatal.

Even without having binged on Game of Thrones and having watched Khal Drogo fade away, she knew, without medication, Dominic would die.

She glanced at Declan. "I'm worried."

He nodded. He looked like hell. His handsome face was drawn and shadowed. His hair was a mess. "As am I."

"He needs penicillin."

"What is that?"

"It's a common drug in my time."

Declan froze. His face paled and his throat worked. "Your...*what*?"

Oh fuck. She hadn't intended to say that. "I mean, in my country."

"You said *my time*."

She offered a toothy smile. "You misheard me."

"I know what I heard." His eyes went flinty. "Are you from some other realm? Some other time?"

She plucked at a hem. Shrugged. "Maybe?"

He crossed his arms and stared at her. He hummed with intensity. "Does Dominic know?"

"I...ah... Know what?"

"What you are? What you really are?"

"Yes."

He stilled. "Does he...accept it?"

"I think he does." She set her hand on Dominic's. It was scorching. "We were just making peace over it when he was injured."

"Where do you *really* come from Maggie from Seattle?" There was a thread of a sneer in his voice.

"Oh, I do come from Seattle. But Seattle about seven hundred years from now."

His jaw dropped.

"Yeah. I was as surprised as you to find myself here."

"How did you do this?"

She shrugged. "It wasn't on purpose, I assure you. I simply stepped into a stone circle back home and landed in yours."

"The stone circle. Is it some kind of magical place?" This he asked with the tone of a man who didn't believe in magical places. Then again, neither had she. Until now.

"Probably more of a temporal displacement."

His lashes flickered.

"Listen, Declan, if I can get back home, I can get the medicine Dominic needs. I can save his life." Hope, excitement, rose in her breast. "Please Declan. Can you take me back there? Back to the circle?"

"Aye." His eyes narrowed. "But what if you get home, and you decide you doona want to come back? Doona want to save him?"

Her heart clenched. "I will come back," she rasped through a raw throat. "I have to save him. I can't live without him. I...love him."

For the first time, his harsh expression softened.

"I want to stay here. With him. Forever."

A pity she didn't know if Dominic wanted the same.

Hopefully, if her plan worked, if she could get home and being back the medicine he needed, she could save him. And she would have a chance to ask him.

And if he said no...well, she'd deal with that when the time came.

* * *

She and Declan left as soon as they could, leaving Ewan with Dominic and making him promise he would not let the doctor into Dominic's rooms. The ride back to the hunting camp took much less time than it had in the cart. Within two hours, at a fast pace, they'd traversed the valley. Though they'd been riding hard, there had been time to talk, and she and Declan had come to some semblance of peace.

She even told him of her home on the hill, her cousin, Jenny, her grandmother and the horrific dog that had started all this. She complained again about having lost her locket that day, when he hefted her over his shoulder.

That he laughed did not help her outrage.

They found the *ciorcal cloiche* with no problem whatsoever. But as she stepped between the stones, Maggie didn't feel it, the sizzle she'd felt before.

She whirled around, arms out, willing the magic to happen.

But it did not.

There was nothing.

Not so much as a whiff of it.

"I don't know what I'm doing wrong," she said.

Declan stood just outside the circle so as not to interfere with her magic—such as it was. "Try recreating your movements."

Maggie closed her eyes and tried to remember. Chasing the dog. Trying to catch him and then…

A chuckle filled the clearing. She stood and glared at Declan. He crossed his arms and tipped his head to the side. "Were you doing some kind of dance?"

"No. I was trying to catch the dog. And then my locket fell off and I bent to grab it—"

"This locket?" he asked, stepping forward and picking up the gold chain. The heart caught the light and flashed.

"Oh yes. That's it—"

But she was speaking to no one.

For just then, Declan disappeared, and the locket with him.

CHAPTER TWELVE

MAGGIE STARED IN HORROR AT THE SPOT DECLAN HAD BEEN.

With him, her only chance of saving Dominic had vanished as well.

Oh, why hadn't she taken the time to look for the locket first? She should have known it was some kind of key.

Who knew where Declan had gone. What if this portal worked willy nilly, spitting out travelers hither and yon with no rhyme or reason? Jenny had mentioned something about unstable wormholes but for the life of her she couldn't remember what it was.

She dropped down on to a mossy hillock and wiped the tears from her eyes.

She'd really screwed things up.

First of all, she'd changed history and Liam had been killed.

Who knew if Jenny was still alive? If she ever had been?

Second of all, Dominic was at death's door with an infection that could have been cured in days if she'd had the sense to bring him along.

Why hadn't she thought to bring him back to Seattle with her?

Granted, he might not have survived the ride here, but still.

And finally, even if he did survive, she had to face him and confess to losing his beloved brother to some temporal beast that gobbled up anyone with the misfortune to wear a heart shaped pendant.

It was tragic.

Truly it was.

With a sigh she stood. She should go back to the castle. Sit with Dominic.

Even if Declan did make it to Seattle, he wouldn't know where to go, or what to do to get the medicine his brother needed. And even if he succeeded, it could take a long time—days, maybe weeks—for him to complete the mission.

Dominic did not have that much time left.

She wanted to be with him while she could.

And it did occur to her that—whether he lived or died—she was stuck here now. The thought of being here without him was unendurable.

A sound behind her snared her attention. She whipped around. Her legs nearly collapsed when she saw Declan, standing there, with an enormous duffle bag over each arm. He was wearing a pair of jeans and a Seahawks jersey. His hair had been styled and his beard trimmed into an adorable scruff. He grinned. "I'm back."

"But you just left," she breathed.

He nodded and walked through the stone circle. "Well, that's a temporal aberration for you. When traveling through time, time itself becomes irrelevant."

She gaped at him. Those words...so familiar...

"Oh, Jenny says hello."

"You saw her?"

A flush rose on his cheeks. "Aye. She helped me get the medicine we needed."

She took one of the duffels from him and they headed for the horses. "What else did you bring back?"

"Lots of things. She thought you could use a care package." He reached into his pocket and handed her an orange-wrapped candy bar.

God bless Jenny.

When they reached the horses, Declan stilled. He turned to her. His throat worked. "Maggie of Seattle. I owe you an apology,"

"You owe me nothing."

"I do. I do. I was...what word did she use? A douche canoe."

Maggie's eyes widened. "Did Jenny call you a douche canoe?"

He grimaced. "More than once."

Poor guy. "She's a tough nut."

"What does that mean?"

"She's hard to get. You know a woman who's difficult to win."

His flush rose higher. His lips curled. He turned away to load the bags on the saddles. Maggie's suspicion rose.

"How long were you there?" She had to ask. She had to know.

"Two weeks."

"I see." He helped her into her saddle then mounted himself. He grunted and adjusted his jeans; probably not used to riding in skin-tights.

"And you and Jenny?"

He flinched. "What?"

"Did you..." she flourished a hand.

His ears went pink, giving her the answer she needed.

"Ah... Did you get the penicillin?"

He blew out a relieved breath. "Aye. Oh aye."

"Excellent. Then let's go. Dominic should start a course right away."

"Aye." He set his heels to his horse's flanks. With some surprise she realized he was wearing Air Jordans.

But one thought roiled in her bemused mind.

Declan and Jenny…

Imagine that.

* * *

Dominic emerged from a black fog aware of a sharp pain in his chest and fur on his tongue. He could hear bickering, and the last thing he remembered was engaging in a brutal battle with his greatest enemy, so he thought it best to lie still and listen.

"Nae. 'Tis far too risky." Ah. Declan. Thank God he was here.

"Risky? Doing nothing is far riskier." His heart thumped in joy to hear Maggie's voice. That she was bellowing at Declan was good too. "Honestly, Declan. What do you have to lose?"

"Half our crop?"

"Or all of it? If you wait too long the rains will destroy everything. What's more, your crofters will die if they're not brought into the castle walls."

"What makes you think the rains will be that bad?"

Dominic cracked open a lid in time to see her waggle a thick tome at his brother. "Because this says so."

Declan frowned and tried to take the book from her. She didn't allow it.

"No. I told you. It's not a good idea for you to know too much about your future."

"That's the dumbest thing I ever heard. What's the point of knowing the future if you canna use the knowledge to keep your people safe?"

"I'm telling you how to keep your people safe, for God's sake. Why do you have to be so fricking stubborn?"

"What does that mean, fricking? Jenny said it all the time."

"Stop trying to change the subject."

It was damn entertaining watching them quarrel. He had no idea why.

Or he did.

The energy between his brother and his woman was just as it should be. A prickling irritation.

He might have chuckled because she turned to him. Her eyes widened and she dropped the book and rushed to his side. "He's awake! Look Declan, he's awake!"

"I see that. Welcome back, brother."

"Welcome back?" The words clung to his throat. Maggie poured him some water and helped him drink—although he needed no help. It was a delicious wash, bathing his throat with cool clear water.

"Ah."

"Aye. We feared we would lose you."

"That bad?"

"Your wound became putrid," Fergus, the doctor, said from somewhere beyond his field of vision. But then, all he really saw was Maggie.

She rolled her eyes. "Ugh. Don't use that term. It's revolting." She patted his shoulder gently. "You had an infection," she said, enunciating each word as though he were a child. "We gave you some medicine."

He frowned at her then shot a glance at his brother, who nodded. "Penicillin."

"What is that?"

"A miracle potion, apparently." Fergus stepped forward, his palms raised to the heavens. "It brought you from death's door in three days."

Maggie frowned at the doctor. "Pish. It's just medicine."

"And where did you get this just medicine?" Dominic asked her.

She glanced at the doctor and pressed her lips together, then murmured, "Um, Declan went to Seattle to get it."

What the hell?

She patted his hand. "We'll tell you all about it later."

"Right," Declan nodded and for the first time Dominic noticed what he was wearing. The same strange breeks Maggie had worn the first time he'd seen her. He opened his mouth to ask...something, but Declan didn't allow him a moment. "Now," he said. "According to Maggie, a great rain is coming. One that will flood the valley. She thinks we should have an early harvest, though if we do that, we will likely lose half our crop..."

He babbled on, but Dominic wasn't listening. Not really. His gaze was locked to Maggie's face as she glared at his brother.

God he loved her.

He needed to tell her.

And he would.

Soon.

With that thought, his exhaustion overcame him and he drifted off to sleep while they squabbled around him.

* * *

He was stronger every day, a fact that made Maggie's heart ache. There was no way she could have the dreaded conversation with him while he was ill...but he wasn't so ill anymore, was he?

Though she desperately needed to know how he felt about *them*, most specifically, if he wanted her to stay, she was frightened to death the answer wouldn't be the one she needed to hear.

That was probably why she put it off for over a week.

Not that they didn't spend time together—they did. Talking, cuddling, kissing. Nothing more, though, because his wound was still healing. She had to insist. Though he was somewhat adamant as well.

He enjoyed exploring all the trinkets Jenny had sent with Declan, enjoyed quizzing Maggie on their purposes. The toilet paper befuddled him, as did Maggie's delight at finding it. He really enjoyed the perfume Jenny had sent, but he was especially intrigued by the Swiss knife and the powerless egg beater drill her cousin had found at a store that specialized in prepping for the Zombie Apocalypse.

But then, men were probably bedazzled by tools no matter the era they lived in.

Dominic was also fascinated with the book Jenny had sent—*The Macintoshes of Dar*.

Maggie came upon him reading it in bed when she went to check on him one morning.

Though the sight of him poleaxed her—beautiful and braw, stark naked on the bed, reading a book, was there ever a more alluring vision?—she attempted a glower. She propped her hands on her hips and growled, "You're not supposed to read that book."

He glanced up at her and grinned. "It's interesting."

She tried to tug it away from him but he resisted. "Come on. *I* want to read it."

He pulled her down by his side instead. Kissed her brow. "You've read it."

"I have. But it's different now."

"The book changed?"

She shrugged. "History changed. We changed it." Fortunately not too much. Liam had not died without sons; her family lineage was intact. And Declan had assured her the Nazis lost the war...and Starbucks still served leaded coffee.

"I like that." Dominic kissed her again. He was so warm, his skin so soft. She regretted her decision to wait until he was fully healed to have him again. "We changed history, you and I." He turned back to the book, opening it to a page near the back and she frowned.

"It's not good to know too much about your future." She knew this. It was an immutable fact. It was brought up in each and every time travel movie she'd ever seen.

"I'm no' reading about *my* future." He curled her against him and pointed to a very familiar photo, a smiling woman in the arms of a very handsome man who stared down at her in adoration. "Did you know this woman made a fortune selling apples?"

She patted his arm. "I do. That's my grandmother. And it wasn't apples. It was Apple *stock*."

"Stock?"

"In 1980, she invested in a small start-up company that made computers—" At his frown, she began again. "A company that made...tools for people." Surely he would understand *that*. "She invested on a whim because she liked the name."

"What was it?"

Maggie winked. "Macintosh."

His chuckle warmed her.

"Anyway, it was a smart investment and it made her very rich."

He flipped back a few pages. "Was there really a world war?"

"Hmm. A couple."

"They sound horrible."

"They were."

"And a man on the moon? And these…cars?"

She pulled the book from his grasp. "It's not a good idea to know too much about the future."

"You keep saying that."

"It's true. Self-fulfilling prophesies, future times, grandfather paradoxes and all that. You don't want to create a rip in the space time continuum."

He ignored her blethering. "You really do live in a miraculous age, Maggie."

Hope flared in her chest. "Would you… Would you like to see it?"

His frown burst her bubble.

"Nae." He forced a smile. "Declan's been telling me about it. How fast things are. About the crowded cities and the stone roadways. The fact that people are no' a *community* anymore." His lashes flickered. "Will you be happy? Going back?"

She stilled. She swallowed heavily. This was it. This was her moment. She met his eye and said, "No."

"Nae?"

"I would no' be happy. Going back. I would rather stay here. With you."

He stared at her. Said nothing, only stared.

Her chest tightened. Her lungs locked. A cold wind howled through her soul "But if that's not what you want, I'll leave of course. I'll—"

"You are no' leaving me, Maggie-mine. Not ever." His expression went fierce. His nostrils flared.

Oh lord. She loved his ferocity. She loved his snarl. She loved him, her highland warrior. "What are you saying Dominic?"

"Do you no' know?"

"I'd like to hear it."

"Then I shall say it. You willna leave me, Maggie-mine, because I love you. Need you. Cannot bear to face life without you by my side. And..." A glimmer danced in his eye. "Because you're carrying my son."

Her eyes widened. "I...am?"

"Aye. According to this book you love so much." He flipped through the pages and found what he was looking for. "He will be born in April. And his name will be Steve."

"Steve?" Her joy, her elation fizzled into bewilderment. She wrinkled her nose. Why on earth would she name her baby Steve?

"Aye. Steve Jobs of the Macintosh Clan."

"It does not say that." She snatched the book from him and scanned the page. And lord have mercy. It did.

She also saw, before she had a chance to look away, that there would be many more children coming from this union. And that she and Dominic would both live long and happy, healthy lives and —

Dominic smacked the book closed and shot Maggie a blistering, hungry stare.

Enough reading. He had other thoughts dancing in his head. He was feeling stronger, and she was here in his bed, and it had been far too long since he'd had her.

He tossed the book to the floor and pulled his woman into his arms.

Oh no. She would not leave. Not ever.

She opened her mouth to protest, or to say something at least. It began with, "I love you t—"

Whatever it was, it was not as important as the message he needed to give her.

Without a word, he settled his mouth over hers.

He kissed her for a long, long while.

And more.

Also by Sabrina York

CONTEMPORARY

Stand Alone
Heartbreak on a Stick (Contemporary Romance)
Pool Man (Sexy Vacation Debacle)
Whipped (Contemporary Romance)
Fierce (One Night Stand, Decadent Publishing)
Snow Angels (Calendar Men Series from Decadent
Publishing)

Stone Hard SEALs — Action Adventure Romance
Stone Hard SEALs (Action-Packed Military Romance Duet)
Guard Dog (Stone Hard SEALs/Hot SEALs Crossover)
Herding Cat (Stone Hard SEALs/Hot SEALs Crossover)
Hot Rod (Omega Team)

Stripped Down Cowboys (And Prequel Novellas)
Stud For Hire, Book 1
Cowboy to Command, Book 2
Spurred On, Book 3

Prequel Novellas
The Real McCoy Prequel Book 1
Come Hell or High Water Prequel Book 2
Protect and Serve — Cowboy Justice 12 Pack Prequel Book 3

Tryst Island Series — Steamy Contemporary Romance
Rebound Book 1
Dragonfly Kisses Book 2
Smoking Holt Book 3
Heart of Ash Book 4
Devlin's Dare Book 5
Parker's Passion Book 6

About the Author

Her Royal Hotness, Sabrina York, is the New York Times and USA Today Bestselling author of hot, humorous stories for smart and sexy readers. Her titles range from sweet & sexy to scorching romance. Visit her webpage at www.sabrinayork.com to check out her books, excerpts and contests.